SONG TO THE RISING SUN

SONG
TO
THE
RISING SUN

A COLLECTION

PAULETTE JILES

POLESTAR
BOOK PUBLISHERS

Published by
Polestar Press Ltd., R.R. 1, Winlaw, B.C., V0G 2J0, 604-226-7670

Distributed by
Raincoast Book Distribution Ltd., 112 East 3rd Avenue,
Vancouver, B.C., V5T 1C8, 604-873-6581

Published with the assistance of the Canada Council
and the British Columbia Cultural Services Branch

Canadian Cataloguing in Publication Data
Jiles, Paulette, 1943-
Song to the rising sun
ISBN 0-919591-45-0
1. Title.
PS8569.I4S6 1989   C813'.54   C89-091627-6
PR9199.3.J54S6 1989

Acknowledgements
Thanks are due to the supportive people at CBC, including John
Juliani, Geraldine Sherman, Eithne Black, and Katherine
Ashenberg; to Caroline and Jeff, Lorraine and Bill, and Gillian
and Joan in Nelson for their help during travels;
and to Connie Rooke, Julian Ross, and Jim Brennan.
"Song To The Rising Sun" first appeared in *The Malahat Review*;
"Badlands" in *The 1989 Macmillan Anthology*.

Design and cover illustration by Jim Brennan
Produced by Polestar in Winlaw, B.C.
Printed and bound in Canada

This book is for Jim , with love

CONTENTS

RADIO WORK: AN INTRODUCTION

There is a very big difference, for me, between work written for radio and work that I think will never leave the page except during readings. This century is the first century in our history in which one can hear poetry and not be in the presence of the speaker. We can sit alone without others, without being part of a body called "audience," and receive poetry or drama without having to give anything back to a living presence. There is no eye contact, no release and pause as the chorus comes on with massed voices, freeing us from the intensity of the single performer or the monologue. But I wanted to go back to those older devices. Just because you or perhaps one or two others are sitting there unseen by me or by the actors is no reason not to use these techniques.

Geraldine Sherman, whom I had earlier worked with as a freelancer for CBC Radio in Toronto, asked me if I would like to contribute a work written for radio, for "State of the Arts," in the summer of 1985. All those years of doing radio work to support myself while I scribbled poetry at night, and finally the two came together! It was old home week. I wrote a piece called "Oracles" and inveigled three friends into going up to the Ainsworth Hot Springs' caves (near Nelson, B.C.) to wade around with me in the hot water and intone poetry like the Delphic Mermaids. We got dripped on and strangled by steam, so that didn't work. Never mind, I said, on to Cody Caves—just up the mountain a little way. Some more forging on, carrying flutes and recording equipment and the inevitable dog, and we managed to record the frame: myself, Caroline Woodward, Joan Webb and Megan Baxter. The CBC technician in Vancouver winced a little as he listened to the quality of the tape, but it passed.

I have always had an interest in the radio audience. When I was putting together documentaries for CBC Radio in the early '70s, I would listen to the producers talk about the size of audiences for different shows. I would read letters written by listeners in far places. I would interview people over phone link-ups as far away as Beirut. It seemed to be an audience that was bigger than, but yet included, the reading audience for poetry. One seemed, somehow, to be more in the presence of the radio audience, and I liked that. The audience appeared to be flexible, interested, alert — an audience that responded with vitality. The sense of a non-hostile audience can bring the best out of a writer or a performer.

After imagining "Oracles" and seeing it actually happen in the studio and on air, I then had the opportunity to do more radio work. This came under the direction of John Juliani, a very supportive and talented director. In this rich atmosphere of sound effects, music, and actors' voices, I found the categories of possible works expanding for me. Material that has lain long unused — when it had to be ground through a typewriter strictly for the page — began to find its form and voice. Experiences and thoughts about the Arctic, about a journey through Morocco, about family histories — all arrived ready to take their place in the creative world. And it was fun; sheer fun. As I wrote the pieces, I began to be able to hear them happening. I knew where I wanted my actors: close to the mike, far off, shouts, whispers, noises, low music, clocks ticking, massed voices, a chorus. But radio drama was a new skill, and it took some learning.

Radio also gave me a larger arena in which to be dull, in which to fall on my face. I did that a couple of times. But, like the bullfighter who put mustard on his sword, I was always hopeful.

The first radio play I wrote, called "Easy Street," was of what I call the "overheard" type. It works for many people, but I am not good at it. It is a representational style. The action and sound occur on a flat plane which is overheard by the audience, and almost all speech is conversational. Information about what is occuring is conveyed through dialogue. But the next year Juliani asked me to try again, and I thought, Why am I writing this kind of drama if it isn't working for me? And so I invented a narrator who speaks directly either to herself or her soul or, incidentally, the audience — with no interference. I found a chorus, and used the power of massed voices and, in "My Grandmother's Quilt," the voice of a spirit. In "Money and Blankets" the voice of a spirit, The King Of The Rattlesnakes, is also present. I learned what you have to do with choruses and spirits is just haul them in without explanation. You don't have to explain nervously about it being in a dream, or coming out of the character's imagination — be bold, be insane, just chuck it in. And then, of course, it has to work.

"Song To The Rising Sun" uses very old devices: repetition, variations in sentence structure, those long series of driving imperatives, the fall-back into a softer lyric, the direct address to the audience, and doubled or chorused or massed voices. In university I would hear my professors expound on *The Odyssey*, and the techniques the poet used, and how brilliant they were, and I could never figure out why poets or writers weren't using them now. So I used

11

them. It makes the poetry more dramatic. It gets contrasty, as the photographers say, and the truth is, you can use anything you want.

A final consideration about poetry that is written to be heard is time. It happens within a certain amount of time which is controlled by the speaker of it. It truly asks for a suspension of disbelief in that the audience is asked to give over its control of time to the writer/speaker, and the audience is required to abandon that solitary, individual control which each member of it would have over a book in one's hands. I don't know how important this issue of control is: perhaps we simply wish to surrender as little control as possible in our lives. So, when you are reading these things you will have to fill in the soundscapes yourself, alone there with the book.

SONG TO THE RISING SUN

Dedicated to Caroline Woodward

1

What did we do all winter while we waited for the sun?
It was gone such a long time.
Our thoughts grew too vague to contain.

What did we do all that winter in the Arctic while we
    waited for the sun?
The stars never stopped looking down at us.
What did we do as we moved into the precise and surgical
    cold of January?
What did we do?
We listened to the radio, we listened to the seductive
and fraudulent voices,
we listened to the voices of pilots overhead in the dark,
we listened for the call sign of the criminal devils
at the Black Angel Lead and Zinc Mine,
we watched with fascination and dread
the talking heads of television from distant places,
we drew up plans,
we cut our losses,
we re-read our contracts,
we visited everybody in the village,
we dreamed,
we were dreamed,
we looked again and again at the southern mountains
behind the village
where the sun would come up,
we talked ourselves out of despair,

we deceived each other,
we traded clothes,
we ran the huskies out from under the staff house,
we wrote eyewitness reports,
we wrote appeals to get our friends out of jail in Kuujuuak,
we invented relationships,
we became deft and scandalous,
we listened to the breaking and the cannonades
of the moving ice,
the destruction of ice at the shear zone,
we arose in the dark and saw angels walking with candles
under the landfast ice, through the caves and tunnels
under the landfast ice,
we watched beings walking down from the southern
mountains in glowing zodiacal bituminous fires,
beautiful and shoeless,
we lay back in our beds, starfire descending.
The spirit sings.
The spirit sings.
The spirit also weeps.

14

2

I have been trying to reach you by radio all winter
but the air is full of darkness,
telepresences, moving stones, talking heads, wizards,
devices, shaky people moving without hands,
devices, radio waves, refuelling aircraft.
I sit up late, listening to Shaman Radio.
The seductive and fraudulent voices tell me of murders
in far places, committed with enthusiasm and skill.
I do not know why the human mind pauses in
the darknesses it does.
But mine has as well.
I drink so deeply of the crystalline and windless stillness
but there is no still place for this thirst.

3

When I first came up here
I came up on a Twin Otter, a cargo plane
carrying four barrels of aviation fuel.
I like living on the edge.
We flew over the Black Angel Lead and Zine Mine
at 8,000 feet,
and the stories the pilot told me were always full of money.
Junk is lethal.

We flew through a thickening, dirty pollution haze
that comes up from the megacities.
Junk is lethal.
He said once his cargo door flew open and he lost
all these boxes of apples
over the Davis Straits,
and he said, you know,
I think Big Stuff will save us.

4

I am trying to reach you by radio.
Listen. Take thought, take thought, think. Listen. Watch.
I am trying to reach you by radio telephone,
waiting for the sun to come back.
I wanted to tell you
we don't have very long.
We are losing things.
There is a black hole in the ionosphere
out of which lost things are going.
We dreamed.
We were dreamed.
I became far too involved with the man
who was ruined; who had a love of
intrigue and whiskey, as did I; lost things are going.
There are 100 million tons of sulphur dioxide
staining the polar air
into a haze that pilots cannot fly through.
Junk is lethal.
We are waiting out the long Arctic night.
The air is overloaded with signals.
In the eastern Arctic, the air is dirty with signals.
Brand names, long wave, short wave, the morse of
supply ships coming up the Davis Strait with their cargoes
of summer fuel
and dreaming sailors
dreaming up the long straits
and the heart's charged cargo spills the entire load out
8,000 feet over the Davis Straits
spilling its dirty hearts, and the
haunting, flaccid little poems we all used to write.
Junk is lethal.
Junk is lethal.

17

What you really want is whatever is really big and comes from someplace else that isn't here and can only be operated by trained experts and is made up of complex components that can only be repaired in Zurich and displaces trillions of cubic feet and is image-intensified at a rate of twenty thousand pounds per square inch and can deal with four thousand feet of unconsolidated sediments and the buildup in terms of p.s.i. whatever has digital readouts. yes. yes. yes. yes. it has to have digital readouts.

Wake up and start again.
Wake up and free yourself.
You must be told this over and over, in dreams,
in messages, in radio waves.
There is more than this, even though the darkness
is seductive with points of light,
snow refractions,
even though there are angels walking under the landfast ice;
you are sick with power
you are sick with the deep acids of power
heavy metals washing ashore,
even though there are beautiful and shoeless people
moving in bituminous fires through the aurora borealis,
even though the legendary stars move in circles
around the high centred polestar
there is more than this. There is more than this long night.
You must be told this over and over.
Wake up. Wake up. Look to the southern mountains,
look beyond the river of Salluit,
look beyond the Kuujuuak, the Povungnirtuk,
Big Stuff will not save us. Wake up. Look. Keep watch.

5

You were promised something.
You were promised that the sun would come back
out of the long Arctic night.
You were promised clear air, clean water.
It was promised that you would be loved
and they owe you, remember that.
Listen to Shaman Radio, listen
to this seductive and fraudulent voice;
they promised you the way the sun makes promises
to the moon
even when the moon is on the opposite side of the world
even when the moon has gone down into the running stains
of the Black Angel Lead and Zinc Mine
even though the sun has abandoned us and left us
in darkness for so long,
promises like the cheerful kisses
of the saffron poppies of the Ungava.
Trust yourself, says the invisible sun, trust me,
trust the light that may rise within you all winter
time after time
following the route of the invisible sun
the moon our representative
the refuelling aircraft arriving on the sea ice,
trust yourself and the light that may rise within you
beautiful and shoeless
down the long alleys of ice at the shear zone
the glitter of accumulated village snow,
and everything I saw in the Arctic and everything I did
became a part of me.
This is my body of darkness and this is my cargo of light.
I was heavy with my body of darkness,
I ride with my cargo of light.

6

And what are the standards set for this sunlight
that has been promised us?
That it be clear.
That it be freely given.
That it fall on everybody at the same time.
That it open our hearts of darkness.
That it illuminate the caves under the landfast ice.
That it give solar power to angels.

That it rise instantaneously over the rim of the southern
     mountains,
that it burst like floodwater down the fjord,
that it set alight and inflame the broken ice at the shear zone,
that it repair and mend our angry, flaccid little hearts,
that it ignite the plankton under the sea ice,
that it make the poppies flare and glitter on the stone tundra,
that it bring the huskies out from under the staff house,
that it draw the birds forward on their great migrations,
that it signal the caribou of the dwindling Ungava herd,
that they shake themselves,
that the hair fly up around them in a bright luminous cloud
as they shake themselves
and prepare to cross the rapids of the Kuujuuak,
that it turn on cloud-shadows over the opening sea,
that it awaken love and foxes.
These are the standards of sunlight.

7

And so we drift out of the precise, surgical cold of January.
We had been dreamed alive,
out of the wreck of the future
out of the violence of opposites
our dreams washing over us all the Arctic night like the tides
under the landfast ice,
running up the Ungava coast in foam and black salt
the routines of oppressive and heavy metals
the heavy metals now in our flesh
now and forever in our flesh
and in the flesh of our people,
and in the flesh of the animals we have dreamed.

8

We always knew we were somebody else
as well as the people we have become.
Something is dreaming us, as persons of intelligent purity,
an evocative and spontaneous self.
We would like to meet this self
in a landscape with Arctic herb-willow blossoms
and the saffron northern poppies
and peregrine falcons overhead,

their airy voices light as shortwave,
walking through these dreams in mortal terror
here on the planet of our birth
here in this polar region
we live through profound experiences
every moment of our lives
every second of our lives,
and we do not know it.
You are right to live in fear.

9

We have to walk on earth as if we lived here.
There is no help for it.
Even if we can only pretend we live here.
They are a small people, but hardy and truthful.
Moving on faith alone.
In the hot moonlight and drifting black shadows,
you are right to live in joy, but
do not meddle in the ways of wizards
for they are subtle,
and quick to anger.

10

And every dream is an explorer's map recovered at great cost
and every map is a chart for land-dancing,
and every river is a song driven by longing
but be still. Sit down here beside me.
Look at the southern mountains,
because this is the opening chord of the music,
because even the darkest heart can be opened,
because the sun can move across the limb of the south
without our help,
because the only changes we have made here
were the wrong ones,
because we have torn a hole in the ionosphere,
because we are pouring out 100 million tons
of sulphur dioxide a year,
because we have soaked the Arctic pole in a pollution haze
that pilots cannot fly through,
because we have blamed it on everybody else,
because we have said poetry will be only
small lyrics of pastoral love,
because this Arctic sun will open your body on its rising,
because your heart is the sun of the world,
because the sun rises and rises over the bare mountains,
the tundra,
the iron cross on the mountain of Salluit,
because the peregrine falcons are coming back,
their airy voices light as shortwave,
because I am trying to reach you by radio,
and because in the heart of this midnight
there is a sun of the upper air,
because of the bituminous fires, the beings beautiful
and footloose,
because the sun is arriving over the bright ice of the fjord,

because it was promised us that it would rise,
because we were torn apart into lightness
and dark in our original natures,
because we were torn in half,
because the rising recreates us,
because the rising recreates us
just this second
and no more.

A TOURIST EXCURSION TO THE BADLANDS

On The Way

Along the way advertisements will insist you do something;
eat, or surrender, back off from the bluffs, sleep,
go forward, undress, invest in something, catch a flight
to Minneapolis or Butte, have an adventure in an
abandoned mining town. Take heart; ahead is the
REPTILE GARDENS, and the apple, and the expulsion,
and the whole damn show.

Along the way are cattle sales; the panicked ranchy calves
with similar big eyes all looking in double units, the
apostolic auctioneer searching the crowd of hats for
converts, the riders back in the pens wearing antennae
on their galloping heads. You ask yourself, will I never get
to the Badlands, or the REPTILE GARDENS, with all the
distractions and fooling around? Fooling around the bed
full of bedsheets in the cowboy motels, travellers in hats
like flying minds on their way to *les liasons dangereux*.

And on your way to the Badlands every night you can stop
at western bars, change sliding down the old walnut
counters like lost silver children, and the army-colored
pennies, and listen to the heavy and soft musician's
weapons of melody and chord, playing out their
hidden agenda.

And I know these musicians work harder at their sorry art
than I ever in my life have worked at poetry, and take
more personal risks, and are paid about the same, all told.
All told,

you get handtooled by life and its graving instruments,
marked by odd, random designs which can't possibly
mean anything unless seen from an altitude of 1,000 feet,

and so sometimes our lives look like a REPTILE GARDEN,
a roadside attraction on the way to Hell's Half Acre.

The musicians in the fake-adobe bar open their instrument
cases and from time to time remain completely silent.

Park Service Brochures

Grey clouds go running by, herded by thunder,
ruined and torn,
and sunlight flashes out between them
over the Badlands
as if somebody was throwing it out of a drawer

and the chest of drawers was in an empty room
and the room was in an abandoned house
the color of brushed steel
and the high Dakota wind was banging the doors shut
and open and shut again
bouncing styrofoam cups hellbent for apocalypse.
I dreamed last night
you lay beside me
and said, "Honey, I'm going back
home to Corpus Christi."
The Parks Service has left brochures
with the names they give the canted earth
and its layering business,
describing the way
whole gullies have sat down to rest
on the bones below:
— and this is the extract of vermillion
— this is the aperture of the world's eyebone
        spying out at the ridges of baking powder

with ash icing and red "happy birthday dear Badlands"
stripes on them,

the gold sequin parts shaped like ovens
and people hoarding unspent light
unliving their lives in the pressure
of dark talk

who try and try to unshutter,
who are looking for the Goodlands

after all the divorces and the wars, who have been silly
and mad and spendthrift, forgetting their birthdays,
losing their way home from foreign countries, who get into
cul-de-sacs and desert highways, who pray without thought
to whatever divinity comes along, the One that looks like a
Soft Touch, the One that appears the most Tender-Hearted,
or who has the most Coins in its Pockets, the One who
would pull you through the REPTILE GARDENS and the
stretches of the bony country; but you are already in it
and what pressure forced you here, what gambles?
Let us suppose we are people walking across the Badlands.
We are for sure those people walking across the Badlands,
watching the big pearly ridges of buff and opal for hawks,
pulling all our lives behind us, baggage trains,
and these are my brains
which have siezed at everything with dry plans
and maps and calculations
how to get out of here,
and I have come so far in my life
and have loved nothing but my life
until now,
and I think I will begin to rain on this place
until I am empty
or it gives over.

The Goodlands

YOU ARE HERE ⟶ •   aren't you?

And from here you have to invent the Goodlands, because
there is no other place to go, unless you are going to just
sull up and sit here, like a calf in the pens ready to go to
pieces, jammed up in the crowding alleys; you have to
keep on and walk out of the bad standing water rimmed
white as an eye with alkali

toward a river in its own alluvial body, between two sets
of mountains, the Wind Rivers, the Bighorns, a valley with
swales and the weird batty machinery of ducks going
through the air like roaching shears, and all the paths along
the river plated with October leaves, the salt cedar yellow
as Crayolas;

cottonwoods throwing their leaves of large denomination
out over the crowded world, as if the Pope of Jupiter would
arrive in a Starmobile and bless the bowing peasant grass;

all the grass of the valley and the benches, the buffalo grass
and the little short grasses with curly starter knobs and the
level-headed grasses holding up gemwork stems, and the
tall ones in the swales, also bowing, wet-footed;

your mind is a nation, populated with standing armies,
post offices, reptile gardens; and some parts are a wilder-
ness and other parts are dark as railroad clinkers, and
parts are a valley like this where we are going, dreaming
about going someplace, not home, but one parsec to the
side of it;

many people have died to hold this place, they are still finding pieces of coin and horse in Medicine Tail Coulee. But this is why we eat and keep up our strength; to cross into Montana, like people without papers, or reasons, without a fixed address, people at large, expendable nomads, jingling with coins and horses, into the valley of the Little Big Horn, thinking, we could have dinner there. We could win this time.

THE ORACLES

And then what happened?

There is a road leading to the horizon
and at the edge of the horizon is a house.
There are five windows in the house
and the chimney-smoke leads upwards
toward a planet or star.
Behind the house is a path leading into the mountains,
the path crosses stream after stream
and all the streams are leading southwest toward a river.
The path leads to a high pass in the mountains
and at one point a smaller path turns off into
the heavy forest
and is leading toward a cave.

Yes. And then?

Back at the house on the horizon
where the path began, somebody is shouting:

Don't do it!
Don't do it!
I told you a million times not to go that way!
I won't be responsible, I'll tell them that you...

The path is leading to a cave entrance
and the cave entrance is leading downward
into the heart of the mountain,

into the earth,
and the bones buried in the earth
and the song buried in the bones;
songs of love,
songs of desire,
songs of mistaken identities.

And the tunnel went on, leading
to an underground waterfall
and I could hear voices,
they were laughing and talking,
the talk was leading up to something important,

and I said: HELLO?
Do you know which tunnel
leads out of here?

THE ORACLES

You could walk all around this cave
and not find anybody but us.
Somebody got out last year; that was
you, we think.
We're a Sister Act: we call ourselves
        The Oracles.
We are smooth and slightly wet.
This is the end of the West and the beginning
of many strange occurrences
sometime after midnight.
Our caves are just outside the margin of your photographs.
There she is and   there we are.

One Sister *(for Sunny)*

One sister will always be fat and the other one thin.
One sister will look good in yellow and the other one won't,
and the one who doesn't look good in yellow
won't be able to carry a tune, either.
Who took my yellow dress?
Who borrowed my blue shoes?
Susan Marie, you took my 100 percent real silk scarf
and you didn't even ask me if you could borrow it!
Amanda Jean got in my diary and read it, and anybody who
reads somebody else's diary deserves
anything they get.

There will always be one sister who isn't good at math
and one who has wide feet.
The one who has wide feet will be the one who discovers
the drop of blood on the stairs
near the woodstove.
It will be she who knows
that, if you pour wine on it,
the drop of blood will speak
and name the murderer.

One sister will cover for the other one when
the wrong prince shows up, pimply and alcoholic,
with a glass slipper.

(But the story is all wrong! The one with the wide feet
is the one with the delicate skin —
she hid her sister in the laundry basket
because she was so thin.)

There will always be one sister who betrays
the other ones.
Ah, we know whose fault it is.
It's always somebody else's fault;
it's the one who is good at math,
she just can't find her path
in life, she has to work in this roadhouse
carrying trays of beer,
and the other sisters will tell you
she used to sleepwalk in the night
and was once found walking down the railroad tracks
carrying some matches for her daddy
who was a brakeman at that time
for the Burlington and Illinois.

One sister will get divorced and the other one
will stay married forever
and the third one will never get married at all
and will charge a lot of clothes to her account
at a big downtown store.
Dad will always have loved one best and hated one most
and then there was the baby of the family. The family.
The family.
One sister will get married and divorced and have a love
affair in fifteen minutes flat from a standing start
and yet the other one will take all day to
find her hairpins,
only to discover they're all in her hair.
One sister will, at some time in her life, yell
at the other ones:
"You ruined my life! All of you!
You made my childhood totally miserable!"

Then there is the sister who has no sisters
and, in fact, makes them up.
She invents for herself all of the above scenes.
For her, books will open like wicker trunks
full of things she already knew were there
but couldn't get at.
Until now.
It is a delicate cloth, and very old.

One sister will travel to foreign places and see
the Tower of London and the other will take a course
in Mary Kay Cosmetics and then lose all her receipts.
"I never had much luck," she says, from her porch
in Butler County, as she fans herself with a Jesus fan.
One sister will always have had to ride the mule while
the other will get to take Daddy's saddle horse.
The two of them go for the mail like this,
arguing fiercely all the way down Pike Creek Road
"Fair! Unfair! Fair! Unfair!"
Sisters argue like Philadelphia lawyers.

One sister will explain her life in terms of men,
what they have done to her, what they
haven't done to her,
what she wishes they would do to her
or with her, or without her,
and the other sister will listen angrily, tapping her fingers
on the tablecloth.
But they are trying so hard to get along,
so the one who is doing the little number on the tablecloth
gets up to make more coffee and thinks,
"She's still talking about men,"

and this kind of thing will always divide the sisters somehow.
Even though they don't know it.
Zinnias loom with accurate brown looks
out of the garden and their hairdos steam in
the hot sun.
One sister will just have come back from an assignment
in a strange place. There are stamps in weird scripts
all over her passport;
the other one sings in the choir, dazzled by notes.
Why is everybody getting divorced all of a sudden?
It must be something in the water, says the other sister,
the one with the zinnia hairdo.
And the other sister swims across the bay, held up
by blue water. And her sister is drinking
quietly and desperately and continuously
in a northern oil town
and one of the children has fallen off the window ledge.
So the other sister swims with slow determination
from one end of the bay to the other.
It is a matter of liquids,
it is a matter of being held up,
it is a matter of not falling,
it is a matter of keeping on with the swimming motions.

One sister died in the bombardments
and the other sister refugeed with her children
to the countryside. One sister married a tall dark man
and went underground for six months
because she ate his seed, and she liked it,
and zinnias sprouted out of her mouth like words.
Three sisters died in the riots in the square
and the last sister made it to the countryside with

two mattresses, three blankets, four children
and a water container.
One sister married a tall dark man and went underground,
the other sister did not marry a tall dark man
and went underground anyway.
A hundred sisters died in the siege and a few made it
to the countryside and married tall dark men and they all
lived underground.

A thousand thousand thousand thousand sisters died
in the fires and the falling buildings
along with their fathers and their brothers
and their uncles and their mothers
and their children and their cousins
and their neighbors
and the unborn
and the unborn
and the unborn.

THE ORACLES

The woman who said YES
And the man who said NO
Key activities and tasks — do you have
    WORD TROUBLE?
The woman who said LISTEN
And the man who said WAIT HERE
And the man who said WHEN?
And the woman who said MAKE A WISH
Yes. No. Listen. Wait here. Make a wish.
And then, they kept on walking

until they found something
         SQUISHY
lying in the cave...

I Used To Live In The City

Now I live in British Columbia but
I used to live in the city.
People owed me money. I ran around. We read each other's
dissertations and everybody either agreed or disagreed.
Some of us took taxis. There were three flowers on my
windowsill and I never really knew what they meant.
Everything was either true or not true.

In my dreams, early in the mornings, a voice began to narrate
everything that was happening, like a CBC man on the spot.
People came in the door as if they had just arrived from
a parade. Maybe they had. People came in the windows as if
they had just walked out of a wedding photograph.
A barrel race. As if they had just stepped into the picture.
Maybe they had.

My landlady told me:
"The woman who lived here before you ran out on the rent."
And I go, "Is this place, like, you know, safe?"
And she goes, "Yeah, this woman had a parrot named
Walter, she fed it tortilla chips; once she got so drunk
her boyfriend brought her home in a shopping cart. She
used to put pennies on the streetcar tracks and she grew
dope on the fire escape. She said she wrote songs for

a living and sometimes you could hear her crying
in the night."
And I go, "I just want to make sure this place is safe."
And she goes, "Oh, it's safe."
And I go, "You sure?"
And she goes, "Yeah, I'm sure."

Sometimes, when you can't think of anything else to say,
you just
       shut up.

THE ORACLES

You don't remember us, but we remember you.
We see everything in the darkness of the cave.
We remember all the times you made up your mind
and unmade your mind;
we knew about the time you lost your shoes.
And now you want a prediction that makes sense,
clear statements, exact instructions —
and all we can say is
you will probably never find your shoes.
They were stolen by the muse,
and keep on looking for her
because she has your shoes.
Keep on walking.

Following The Muse

I go, ''Is this place safe? I mean, it's kind of
a rough neighborhood.
And my landlady goes, ''Yeah, the woman who lived here
before you, ran out on the rent.''
And she looks at me:

''You don't remember me,'' she goes, ''but I remember you.''
And I remember her.
And every time I see her, she arrives with the news
of starships.
They say she lives on the other side of the mountains.
They say she lives in the ruins of fallen cities
and all-night cafes.

Once I saw her sitting in an abandoned car,
and when she lit her cigarette
the matchlight shone on all the rusty dials.
She's always travelling.
She says, ''You don't remember me, but I
remember you.''
I saw her yesterday at the Salvation Army
trying on shoes that were both
too big, and too small, for her.

She calls you up at one in the morning, collect.
She travels in strange ways,
sometimes on foot.
That was her you saw yesterday at the roadside,
at the Starlight Cafe.
She always seems to have time for things;

for inventions, for pennies on the railroad tracks.
A locomotive comes thundering down on her money.
This is what she does with her money.
She's always travelling.

I promised her everything I have
and she took it.
This is the way she is.

This is the way it is.
Rain falls in a still place,
beside the railroad track;
where you left your money.

THE ORACLES

You can understand all these predictions
because you are clever, living
by your wits.
And inside of your wits you will start wearing
different kinds of clothes,
like people do when they become mothers.
Begin NOW to separate yourself
out of the several billion events happening this precise moment
in the galaxy,
when the whole city flies off
leaving you with nothing but the universe.
The way out of the cave
is up the waterfall.

So I took the tunnel leading upwards
toward a light; and it was bright
and noisy.
It was like the cabin of an
Air Canada Lockhead jet,
and the captain's voice said
we would be landing in thirty minutes,
temperature sixty-four degrees,
slightly overcast;
thanks for flying Air Canada.

And there was a long escalator
leading toward an airport bus
which took the highway leading out
of the city
which led to a road. And on the road
was a house with a chimney
and smoke leading upwards toward a planet
and somebody sitting in there
listening to a radio.

MOROCCAN JOURNEY

(Note: Europeans and North Americans were
called *Nasrani*—"Nazarene" or "Christian."

THE WOMEN'S CHORUS

This is the story of Ahmad; listen.
Ahmad got caught in the middle of a clan feud
between the Al-Waryaghira and the Ait-Wasised.
He saved his life by running into a house
and laying his hand on the handmill
under the protection of the woman of the house,
and he stayed there for three days.
This was how he saved his life.
Before Islam came here, the people worshipped a sheep.
A sheep! Imagine! A sheep, and Emmama-ni, the goddess
of ruined cities and strayed people, and sign-painters.
We have lots of stories like this,
not all of them have happy endings.
But yours will, Nasrani. If there is somebody left alive
to tell the story,
then that is a happy ending.

Now listen — Ahmad. That was one story.
The other is that there was a saint on the mountain,
Jbil Hmam,
and some other Nasranis came through here once.
They laughed when we told them about the miracles
he did for people.
They laughed at us! Hmmm. And then, they got sick.
One of them died.
Have you been laughing at saints, Nasrani?
Hmmm? Have you been laughing at saints?

THE TRAVELLER

Walking east, and then northeast,
we came into the mountains.
And every day we walked further into the secret hemisphere
and every day our loads grew heavier
and every night in the village taverns the men played
at a game
on a board, around the fire,
they were moving pieces on a board;
and so we walked forward, into the Rif Mountains of
northern Morocco, toward Ketama.
We went through Bab Taza, and Meknoul and Bab Berrad.
I put down my pack wherever I found some space;
there was space everywhere.
There was a lot of space.
We travelled and got thinner.
It was Ramadan, the new moon like the jewel of Islam.
But it was a pretty thin moon.
Pretty hungry.
Rahmin, bring me a drink of water.
Men sat before the candle flames
moving small pieces over a board,
they were charting my journey to Ketama,
pieces moved on a board,
farther into the mountains,
and every day our loads got stranger and stranger.

I said,
    "Is there a truck going by here to Ketama?"
and they said,
    "Maybe. Maybe tomorrow. There might be an
onion truck."

Slower and slower we travelled into the other world.
And the second stranger that began to walk beside me
was a wild, dreamlike fever.
Snow drove through the holly trees
and the mountains were like silk prints
and it seemed that the teapot began to tell stories,
steamy and dreaming.

46 THE WOMEN'S CHOURUS

This all depends on time
and time depends on geography
and geography depends on gravity
and gravity is what keeps the evil people down in hell
from floating up like mean balloons.
The soldiers come by, looking for bribes,
and so we dynamite the roads here.
You are in another world, Nasrani.
The helicopters come by, looking for hashish.
But the helicopters are heavy and they sometimes crash.
But angels and strangers are light,
light as fever, as typhoid,
we will weigh you down.
We will weigh you down with the sound of a flute
and the stories of wars, and the marriages, and
the betrayals and the sorcery.
We sell hashish by the kilogram. We use it for magic,
to poison enemies, and to get dreams.
They say the Nasrani use it for fun.
Is this true?
For fun?

THE TRAVELLER

I didn't know whether I was going to make it to Ketama or
not. I was about worn out with adventuring. But we were
so far into the maze of this world there was no way out but
back the way we had come, and that was a very long way.
And I thought, well, you know, everybody has their own
geography somewhere, unfolding from inside themselves,
their own planet, and across these planets there are always
strangers, walking, carrying their stories.

THE MEN'S CHORUS

Some people say the world is a china plate,
held up by dragons.
Some people say the world is an egg,
always generating things and the seeds of things to come.
Maybe it is the amniotic fluid of Emmama-ni,
goddess of ruined cities and dental work,
divinity of lost causes and sign painters.
And some people say the world is perfectly full,
a world without strangers or angels or bandits,
peppered over with stars,
bounced through history by a giant
who is perpetually blind drunk.
Geography supplies us with free gravity
and keeps strangers on the surface of the earth as they
travel across it
and keeps all those evil people from floating up from hell
like mean balloons.

A MAN'S VOICE

No, you can't go any farther. You can see she can't go any farther. She has either a fever or an attack of sorcery. She will stay here until she can travel. You see, there is Rahmin, and Fatima Henna, who does people's hair and makes designs on the hands. And Kenza and Aziza, they will take care of her in the women's compound. If she goes on she will die and so she will stay here and that's all there is to it.

THE TRAVELLER

I was born under a lucky sign. I carried it with me into the mountains of northern Morocca like an astral umbrella, into the Rif mountains, the blad-s-siba, the land of dissidence, and fighting, where people carry their tribal stories like umbrellas, and the runners slide through the holly and beech trees with loads of hashish, mysterious and remote.

They said,
  "Don't go there, the mountain tribes are barbarians!"
They said,
  "Those people worship sheep, or some goddess called
  Emmama-ni!"
They said,
  "You'll never come back alive!"
And so, I had to go. I was born under a lucky sign, the sign of the stranger.

THE WOMEN'S CHORUS

We are Berber, we were once the barbarians
at the gates of the city of Nkur,
a city some people only sometimes remember.

We have become blad-s-siba, the land
of fighting and dissidence and tribal wars.
All those people do is fight each other!
Usually over women.

THE TRAVELLER

I was born under a lucky sign, the sign of Aries and fire
and fever. I sit, wrapped in homespun cloaks, in the
women's compound, and all my bones glow like phos-
phorescent candy. I sit and watch the life of the compound
of Mikki Mohammed, outside Ketama, with the light snow
falling, and the cow eating pomegranate rinds, and the
geese in the straw. The women are boiling my clothes in
a copper pot, talking. The snow drifts down, making crisp
noises on the fire.

THE WOMEN'S CHORUS

Oh Fatima Henna, we have not seen you in so long.
Sister, where have you been?
We have so many secrets to tell you.
There have been births and deaths and marriages,
and the tribes, the Al-Waryaghira and the Ait-Wasised
fell to fighting, arguing among themselves.
Their sisters and our sisters arguing,
fighting at the women's market.
Somebody got slammed with a petrol tin.
A gun went off.
Ahmad ran into a house and put his hand on the handmill.
Everybody married the wrong people
and then made up songs about it:
love lost, love gained, love bought, eluded, betrayed,

broken, refused, betrayed, betrayed.
He was a great man, Abdul-Al-Karim, but he was betrayed.

MEN'S CHORUS

And others say the world is an egg, regenerating things,
one thing unfolding, another thing unfolding.
These are the ten most beautiful things:
soap, and henna, and silk,
the plow, and flocks of sheep and swarms of bees
and then the sun and the crescent moon
and horses and books.
These are the ten most beautiful things.

THE TRAVELLER

Rahmin, bring me a drink of water.

THE WOMEN'S CHORUS

A sheep, and Emmama-ni,
the sheep-headed goddess who lives
under the cooking pots, and drinks the broth,
who lives under the teapots and whispers stories
about her ancient city of Nkur
and makes mischief
and gives people fevers.
Emmama-ni, hiding in the fire and the handmills,
dreaming, ecstatic, old.

THE TRAVELLER

The mind will move where it wants to and when
the mind sits down in a warm dry place

the mind heats up its drum
the mind sits beside a window
the mind walks out at sunrise
like a water-spider
the mind moves where it wants to and when;
there are lanterns and fountains in the land of the Almohades
under the Mountain of Doves.

THE WOMEN'S CHORUS

Walk back and go to sleep again, Nasrani,
what we do here is none of your business.
We are arranging marriages.
It is a delicate and complex work
and you have seen of course that Mikki Mohammed
has put aside his good wife for another woman,
that flashy bitch from Bab Taza,
and we are plotting mischief
against Mikki Mohammed.
We will transfer the fever
from you to him.
Now go away, we are making trouble. Hurry up! Go go go go.

THE TRAVELLER

What would we do without strangers?
There are many uses for strangers.
If we did not have them, we would be too much with
each other, we would become tiny and hard.
We would know everything there is to know
and then the world would become perfectly full,
a tight shell peppered over with stars,
and everything would become perfectly known.

The world inside our heads would become so full
of perfectly known things
that it would start to fray out and ravel
and then gravity would give way
and the evil people would start floating up from hell
like mean balloons.
They have taken away my fever and kept it for themselves.
There are always uses for fevers;
tin cans, bits of string, scraps of leather, plastic bags...

THE WOMEN'S CHORUS

Now go away, Nasrani! We are making trouble; go away!

THE TRAVELLER

Rahmin, bring me a drink of water.

THE MEN'S CHORUS

And some people say the world is held together
by conflicting forces:
hashish runners sliding through the thickets of holly,
helicopters falling toward the fields,
road explosions.
The tribes fell to fighting over the hashish money,
the Al Waryaghira and the Ait Wasised,
but it has always been this way, since the age of paradise,
the age of iron after that, the age of clay pots,
the age of vegetables, and then the age of torch singers and
cheap jewelry. And the age of internal combustion engines,
the age of carbonated drinks,
and the age of the French with gunpowder and plastic
and gas.

Abdul-Al-Karim-Al Khattabi was a great man,
but he was betrayed.

THE TRAVELLER

My fever is leaving me,
a stranger going off somewhere.

A MAN'S VOICE

Rahmin, Rahmin...

THE TRAVELLER

I have been watching Mikki Mohammed, it seems to me
he isn't well. He stands outside the women's compound,
looking thin.

A MAN'S VOICE

Rahmin, bring me a drink of water.

THE TRAVELLER

Will Mikki Mohammed go back to his good wife and leave
that flashy bitch from Bab Taza? Will Rashid marry Fatima
Henna? Will the goat have twins? Does Rahmin know that
Kenza is going to sell the cow? The women tell me in
French that when I go home to my country, nobody will
marry me because I am too thin. And so Kenza and Fatima
Henna are making me a surprise present, a thick long
dress, peppered over with stars, that will make me look
fat. I have left them everything: my watch and my gold
earrings, my paper and pens. I came through the age of
iron, and clay pots, and vegetables, and torch singers, and

I will get on an airplane out of Casablanca, the age of internal combustion engines.

THE WOMEN'S CHORUS

Have you been laughing at saints, Nasrani? Have you been laughing at saints?

THE TRAVELLER

The mind moves where it wants to and when
the mind sits down in a warm dry place
the mind heats up its drum
the mind walks out at sunrise
walking down the Silk Road,
the mind is a water-spider, unspinning its stories
one inside the other
and another one inside that, and another one inside that,
and another one inside that...

MY GRANDMOTHER'S QUILT

The old Huffman house outside New Lebanon, Missouri, is small, made of board-and-batten; it has a fireplace for cooking, three rooms downstairs and an attic with a small window. In the 1880's there was still a great deal of original timber on the rolling hills; not all of it has been cleared. The farms of the area are small, because the soil is good, and are mostly self-sufficient. The Missouri, Kansas and Texas Railroad takes the surplus to market out of Otterville, the nearest town. Jesse James is hiding out 150 miles away in St. Joseph, and the most profitable recent crop is mules, to be sold to the U.S. Army. The Lamine River floods out the valley once a year, but it hasn't yet come as far as the Huffman house. The more affluent town ladies in Otterville and Boonville are wearing bustles, would never appear in the street without a hat, and are not concerned so much with getting the vote as getting a cookstove, and wallpaper and a mangle. But these are luxury items and Margaret Johanna Burnett Huffman is a poor widow. Samuel Huffman, who came from Virginia by ox-cart in 1853 and convinced her to come with him, was a fiddlefoot, a storyteller, and a man with no feck whatever. He resisted joining the New Lebanon church because he had been raised in the German Reformed Church of Virginia and was proud of it. The whole community regarded him as standoffish. Maggie Jo had come with him mostly because her Burnett relatives were already out there in Missouri, and there were uncles and aunts to meet her. And now, even though she has seen her children grown and married, she has two more to care for.

55

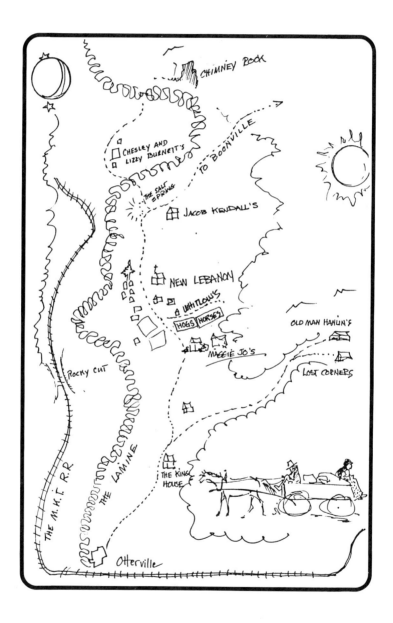

LULA BELLE

The mouth is the place that thoughts leap out of; it is the starting gate of our hearts, where words race out like horses, the words of preachers, whispered conversations, stories told sitting on the rails of the salt springs, the words of fortune tellers. My whole life has been made up out of other people's stories.

The congregation of the New Lebanon church is gathered in the graveyard, under the big pine, to bury Nanni King. Brother Ewing is saying the last words as the red dirt flies.

"Our sister Nancy Elizabeth King leaves behind with us, brothers and sisters, leaves unto our care, two little girls and a grieving husband. The affliction she bore with Christian patience has reached its end, and the soul of Nanni King has gone to dwell in Heaven with Our Lord, who is His infinite mercy gave it, and in His unscrutable wisdom has taken it away. So it is said by the prophet Malachi, chapter four, verses five and six, 'Behold! I shall send you Elijah the Prophet before the coming of the Great and Dreadful Day of the Lord, and he shall turn the hearts of the fathers unto the children, and the hearts of the children unto their fathers, lest I come and smite the earth with a curse.' So here we have the father and the children left to look out after each other, and I know brother King need not fear that warning."

Brother Ewing gives a stiff look at William Nelson King, who is standing there with his hat off, and the two girls clinging to his britches, and the wind up his back. Brother Ewing turns back to the grave and says of his cousin: "And we commend Nanni King's body to the earth, and her spirit will dwell with the Lord."

The congregation sings an old hymn called "Higher Ground," and the wind is still galloping down the Lamine River Valley, snatching at rain and leaves by the handfuls:

Lord, lift me up and let me stand
by Faith in Heaven's table-land...

And the shovels are dispatching dirt onto the coffin and, in the distance, the sound of pigs grunting. Somebody calls out in a desperate stage whisper:

"Chesley Burnett's pigs are out!!"

But the congregation keeps on singing:

A higher plane than I have found
Lord, plant my feet on higher ground...

This is bad news: pigs are known to root up graves, if they can get at them. Maybe they are checking it out; maybe Nanni won't be able to rest in peace.

"Get them damn pigs outa here," says Henry T. Ewing.

"Them's Chesley Burnett's pigs!" says another man.

Somebody slips quietly away from the mourning and hymn-singing and then there is a shot and a squeal and then no more pig sounds.

"Well, Burnett's going to be short one spotted pig, I tell you what."

LULA BELLE
A-women
A-men!
Shot at a rooster and
Killed a hen!

At Maggie Jo's house after the funeral, the girls and their father have come to sink into chairs and commune in broken sentences with one another, stunned as stones. November is a terrible time to lose a wife, a mother, a daughter, and then there were those terrible spying sinister pigs at the funeral. Maggie Jo rocks to the sound of Samuel Huffman's Virginia clock that has a sun and a moon on it and the picture of a lady and a gentleman spooning under a willow.

"Here I am seventy-two years old and still a-living," says Maggie Jo.

"What's that, Mrs. Huffman?" asks William, looking up.

"I don't know why it wasn't me that was took," says Maggie Jo, looking up at the Virginia clock. "It's a full moon."

"Well, if anything should happen while I'm gone, go get Chesley and get him to telegraph me on the Katy," says William, trying to think ahead. He knows he has to leave the girls with their grandmother and take up his brakeman's lantern to supply the money to support this household. Or at least he intends to. "Go to Otterville and send a telegram, Mrs. Huffman."

"What's the Katy, Poppa?" asks Dale.

"That's the Missouri, Kansas and Texas Railroad, honey," says William. "That's where daddy works."

"If anything was to happen, I'd send Dale running over to Whitlow's and tell him," says Maggie Jo, making herself stop dwelling on the pigs and the full moon.

"I'd keep them if I could, Mrs. Huffman," says William, "but you know I won't be home but every three days."

"Grandma? Do I have to run through Whitlow's hog field?" says Dale. She is now permanently afraid of pigs.

"No, honey, run through the horse field," says Maggie Jo.

"That's just if anything was to happen, Dale," says William. "Like you broke a leg or something. And I'd come home right away. Right away. Now, Mrs. Huffman, Brother Ewing is farming your creek land, and Henry T. Ewing will be cutting your timber..."

"Well, she's with the angels now," says Maggie Jo.

"Yes, she is," says William.

"Yes, that's where Mama's at," says Dale, wanting to believe it.

"Where's Mama at?" asks Lula Belle, age four.

"With the angels, Lula Belle," says William.

"Mama is gone with the angels, sister," says Dale, as she suddenly becomes a little mother. It will be a permanent condition.

"Well, when's she coming back?"

"Oh God, children, we do not know when the Grim Reaper will arrive to take us to our final abode!" says William, starting to cry. "A month ago, one night she took all the pins out of her hair and said to me, as I am standing here, she said, 'Mr. King, they say long hair means long life!' Just as I am sitting here. She was beautiful and healthy and ...(he thinks of the words from the newspaper)... accomplished in all the womanly arts, and now she's a-laying in the graveyard. And here's two motherless children. Mrs. Huffman, I am stabbed to the heart."

"Mr. King, take hold of yourself," says Maggie Jo, also starting to cry. "And her out doing a washing in the yard not two weeks ago, a-wringing out everybody's under-drawers."

"Maggie Johanna, Mrs. Huffman, I am going to drive out now. I'm going to Mr. Hanlin's. He will want to hear

Lula Belle and Dale

about the funeral."

"But Poppa," says Dale, jumping up to catch him, "You left your pipe!"

"So I did," says William.

"Poppa, don't go over there," says Dale. "You're just going over there to drink some liquor. Everything in this whole house wants fixin'!"

"Don't tell me what I'm going to do, Dale. My grief is more than I can bear at this particular time."

Old man Hanlin lives on Hess Creek. Chickens roost on his bedstead. He keeps a still and a liquor shop. This is a man's world, over there on Hess Creek; the infamous Lost Corners.

There is rain and distant thunder. It is the spring of 1885. In places, it rains through the old Huffman house. At night the girls lie in their bed up in the attic room and whisper. They have pried up the mill sidings used as finish boards in two places, to keep their small treasures dry, and Lula Belle has discovered that the board-and-battens are a cover over the older house — a log cabin with walnut logs. There is a family of field mice in the old clay chinking. They become her audience, attentive, bright-eyed, rivetted by her scattered thoughts.

LULA BELLE

Me and Dale were born a little while apart. We used to wonder where we came from. We could have been waiting in the clouds of heaven to get born. But then me and Dale started arguing about what kinds of clouds.

A crack of thunder rattles the panes.

I said they would have been thunderclouds, big men-o-war clouds with blazing edges sailing away towards Tennessee. And when the rains come down, it's very tall, like long pieces of jewelry, we could have been wearing the rain for baby clothes, we could have rained on mama in spirits. I mean, our spirits. But Dale said:

63

And the family of field mice all turn to Dale:

DALE

No, it's the clouds like laundry, we could have been washed out of the Holy Washtubs up there!

LULA BELLE

This is big thinking. Me and Dale like Big Thinking, but we only talk it betwixt ourselves, at night, or when we walk down by Hess Creek.

The audience of field mice in the log chinking are suddenly joined, she thinks, by an audience of spotted pigs out in the field. Don't pigs go to sleep at night? She thinks of something else:

We'll be angels after, me and Dale. She says Mama is an angel now.

Maggie Jo looks over at the Virginia Clock. The gentleman and lady, forever fastidiously in love, look down at hands that say ten-thirty.

"Time you girls went to sleep now," says Maggie Jo. "And burn the cobwebs off from over your bed with that candle! But don't you dare burn a spider! That'll mean a death is coming."

Maggie Jo goes back to piecing the "Kaleidoscope" quilt by candle-light. The storm is moving towards them, but slowly. The wind blows up the scent of new leaves and sap rising in the sassafras.

LULA BELLE

I hear mama at night; she taps at the window of Maggie Jo's house, and all the windows of all the houses we be sent to stay at. I remember the time we came down sick. Mama and me had brain fever, we had pneumonia, we swelled up and tossed back and forth in our beds, we lay in a swoon, they cooled our fevered brows and prayed over us both day and night. Mama died, and my mind hasn't been the same as other people's minds since then.

The chorus is made up of Cumberland Presbyterians, a Frenchman in knee-britches with his sword and pistol by his side, a fortune-telling woman, Lucifer, Lula Bell's dear departed mother, sinister pigs, and darling mice:

CHORUS

This unfortunate child Lula Belle King is never going to be right in the head, brothers and sisters, from the outcome and the effects of brain fever, so let her hear what she hears, let her see what she sees. She is not playing with a full deck, she is one brick short of a load. Go to sleep now girls.

"Go to sleep now, girls," says Maggie Jo.
"Goodnight, Dale."
"Goodnight, Lou."

"God bless you, Dale."
"God bless you, Lou."

LULA BELLE

When I first looked at my reader in school, the letters took fire, they swelled up and crossed each other, I got everything backwards. At night there was only one candle on the table, but sometimes I could see two of them, or everybody had holy angel haloes around their heads. I kind of liked it. And I didn't want to learn to read anyhow.

"Now Lou, listen to me," says Dale.

"What?"

"See, this here is an A. See there? It sticks up just like a woodpile."

"'A like a woodpile."

"And this here is a B," says Dale. "Like a pair of big old pillows. Like Aunt Lizzy's bosoms!"

"Like Aunt Lizzy's bosoms!"

"Well, ain't it?" says Dale, drawing another B.

"Yes, and A goes 'aaaahhh" and B goes Buh! Buh! Ah— BUH! Ah-buh! We did that already."

Dale pushes the paper in front of Lula Belle and writes the letters again, B first and then A.

"So, if I write them this way...say the sounds.... I'll give you a hint. What does Maggie Leona's nanny goat say?"

"Baaaaaaaaaaaa!" shouts Lula Belle.

Dale writes the letters again.

"I just wrote that down!" says Dale. "Now read it."

"Abuh," says Lula Belle, squinting at the letters. "It says Abuh. What's a Abuh?"

"How come you're reading it backwards??!!

"Well," says Lula Belle, after a long pause. "Ain't that how it's writ?"

"Grandma Maggie Jo! Come over here and whup this child!" shouts Dale, reaching for Lou.

"Don't you touch me a lick!" says Lula Belle, jumping up. "I'll snatch you bald-headed!"

Maggie Jo leaves off carding cotton and comes to settle things.

"Now Dale," she says. "Sometimes Lula Belle sees things backwards. I've noticed her doing that. But, Lula Belle, see this pattern here? On this quilt?" says Maggie Jo, pointing to the quilt covering her bed over in the corner.

"Double Irish Chain, Grandma," says Lula Belle.

"And that one over there on the trunk?"

"The Drunkard's Path. Ha. Goes from here all the way to Old Man Hanlin's."

"You're walking on thin ice, sister," says Dale, primly.

Maggie Jo goes back to the cotton and pulls a wad loose; picks up more between the carding batts.

"Well, she can read quilt patterns, Dale."

"You little hussy," says Dale, furious that all her efforts have gone nowhere.

"But you can see them all at once," says Lula Belle, looking over at the quilt on the bed.

"Let it go, Dale. Her mind was affected," says Maggie Jo, carding with practiced strokes.

"My mind was affected," smirks Lula Belle.

"If you don't learn to read, they'll take you to the county poorhouse, Lula Belle King."

"Hear what she says, Lula Belle," says Maggie Jo. "Just keep on trying. I never learned to read, and I'm just about in the poorhouse."

"Oh, Grandma," says Dale, "nobody would ever let you go to the poorhouse! Grandma, don't say that. If my mama was here...if my mama was here...

"Hush, Dale," says Maggie Jo. "Tomorrow after school you all go catch crawdads. I don't think studying's too good for your eyes."

CHORUS

Ah-buh! Ah-buh! Ah-buh! Ah-buh!
Old Joe Clark was a preacher man,
he preached all over the plain,
and the only Bible he ever knew
was Ace High, Jack, and the Game.

Old Joe Clark had a yellow cat,
it could neither sing nor pray,
stuck his head in the buttermilk jar
and washed his sins away.

A rig-dum bottom-mitchi-kimbo!
Ah-buh, ah-buh, ah-buh...

Lula Belle and Dale and a cousin, Denver Huffman, have gone to wade in Hess Creek, and balance on the logs that stick out over it, and wonder what they would see if they followed Hess Creek all the way up to Lost Corners.

Denver and Lula Belle are in the shallows, ankle-deep, splashing after crawdads. Lula Belle has on a long dress with her bonnet hanging by its strings, her hair coming out of its braids.

"Put your hand behind him, Lula!" says Denver. "Behind him! They scoot backwards, watch it!"

"I got him, I got him!" says Lula Belle as she fists it up tight in her hand and feels it wiggle and pinch. "Oh, ick, I don't want him. Here Denver, you take him."

Dale watches from the edge, holding his school shoes. The giant willows and sycamore trees brace up a blue sky, grapevines snake down from their branches.

"Eat him, go on Lula," dares Dale. "Crunch him up."

"Eat him, Lula, go on," says Denver. "Crawdads are good."

"I'll eat it, I don't care," says Lula Belle, standing there with the crawdad in her fist, staring defiantly at Denver.

"Go on, Lula, I dare you," says Denver.

"I'll eat it, I don't care."

"Sure, you had brain fever and everything," he says. "You don't know no better."

So she eats it, making crunching noises, pretending to enjoy it. Dale runs out in the creek and tries to open Lula

Belle's mouth to pry it out.

"As God is my witness! She ate it!" says Denver, and begins to imitate Brother Ewing. He addresses a congregation of sycamores:

"Brothers and sisters, cast your eyes upon this afflicted woman! Yes! Afflicted with eatin' things! She's eat things ever since she was a baby! Be healed, woman! Rise up and eat no more!"

"Well, now that I done that, I'm going swimming," says Lula Belle, spitting out pieces of crawdad and splashing water into her mouth. "I'm going to take off my dress and swim."

"Over my dead body you are going to take off your dress," says Dale.

"But Grandma won't find out!"

"I'm just going wading," says Dale. "I don't want people talking about me."

Denver knows neither one of them are going to take off anything. He wants to get rid of them so he can.

"Hey, look — a snake!"

"What? What is it?" says Dale.

"A cottonmouth!" says Denver.

Dale and Lula Belle splash out of the creek screaming and run, then walk, towards home. They wring their hems out, bitching at each other. Lula knows she'll never get to swim naked, not ever, and so she doesn't think about it anymore. Their dresses are uncomfortable, heavy and wet, as they are still wearing homespun, even though almost every other girl in the county now has dresses of machine-woven calico or other cotton. They walk and drip and sigh, pick up Dale's books from a stump beside the road, and go home.

At Grandma Maggie Jo's. Lula Belle is still poking at paper with a pencil now and then, dyslexic, unable to make sense of the scrambled print. She sits beside Dale and cuts out pieces for the "Kaleidoscope," one of the most difficult patterns to fit.

LULA BELLE

Well, Dale reads pretty good now, but I don't read. She reads the Bunceton Eagle out loud to me, which tells all the news around this part of the county, and who got married or born or died or robbed. She saved the paper with mama's obituary on it, which is eight years old.

Dale lays aside her schoolbook and picks up the huge, leatherbound King Family Bible. In Revelations, chapter ten, is a newspaper clipping. Dale reads:

"In the death of Nancy Elizabeth King, which occurred at the family abode as the result of brain fever, near New Lebanon Church, there passed away one of Cooper County's best-loved citizens. By a life of self-sacrificing motherly devotion, Mrs. King always endeavoured to set an example before those who were careless and indifferent to their soul's best interests. The attractive and beautiful Mrs. King was accomplished in all the womanly arts and led an exemplary Christian life, leaving two small girls, Dale Burnett King and Lula Belle King, ages four and six, and a grieving husband, William Nelson King. Mrs. King was twenty-eight."

Lula Belle looks at the familiar clipping and asks, "Was she beautiful or was the newspaper just saying that out of habit?"

Dale holds the newspaper clipping as if it were Holy Writ, between her two hands, but she is looking into the fire.

"She had brown eyes, she had a big heavy head of hair that come out of its pins and fell down to the seat of the chair she was sitting on. She had a looking-glass of silver where she could see how pretty she was, and she used to sing 'Wayfaring Stranger.' Do you like that song, Lou? I like 'Motherless Children' better. It makes me cry."

"Sometimes I like crying," says Lula Belle.

"Me too."

"Sometimes I like just getting right down and howling and bawling," says Lula Belle.

"I like sitting on the sycamore down at the creek and weeping and pining," says Dale.

"Me too. And now, read me 'Jim Drew, Worthless Otterville Negro.'"

Dale groans to herself. She turns the clipping over to the other side and reads: "Alright. 'Jim Drew, Worthless Otterville Negro, Gets Ready For Another Trip To The Penitentiary.' When Ester Lacy, a colored boy from near Belle Aire, came to Otterville Tuesday night, he tied his horse, a three-year-old bay mare, to the hitchrack of Ollie Jones' store. After transacting some business, he returned to find his mount gone. Upon inquiry, he found that Jim Drew was also missing. Now, when Jim Drew gets some bad whisky in him, the first thing he thinks about is getting his hands on something loose. Sheriff Lambert...' And here's where it's torn."

Lula Belle knows that's where it ends but pretends to be disappointed.

"Lou, this paper is eight years old," says Dale.

"You know what?" says Lula Belle. "If everybody in the world wanted it to be 1873, it would be 1873."

Dale thinks about it, and gives up. She says, instead: "Where do you come up with these notions? That's demented."

72

"That Jim Drew, was that the colored man they took out and hung?"

"Where'd you hear that!!??"

"I hear anything I want to," says Lula Belle, satisfied and sly. "I had brain fever. Nobody pays any attention to me."

"I don't know whether it was him or not," says Dale, turning the clipping over again. "That happened on November 29th, 1876, was what I heard."

"So it's not in that paper?"

"It's not in any paper."

Lula Belle takes up the scissors and cuts carefully into an old dress that had been given them by the church.

"You know what?" she says. "I'm going to make a quilt myself, and make it out of old patches from everybody's clothes so that you can see all the stories in it."

"Well, some stories you'd better keep quiet about," says Dale, reluctantly putting the clipping away. It seems another small loss to put it back in chapter ten, and close the heavy bible on it. Lula Belle is off on "that" subject however, and won't quit.

"A bunch of men got drunk and went out and did that. Down by Chouteau Creek. Drunk on Old Man Hanlin's whisky. And where was Daddy, pray tell?"

Dale goes back to her schoolbook.

"Why...why he was off in Otterville, that's where. Look for some nicer stories, Lula."

Lula Belle shakes out the dress she is cutting up. Small bits of hay fall out; timothy seeds.

"Uh-huh!" says Lula Belle. "Maybe here, look, this is one of those Speece girls' dresses, and there's hay in it! She's been up in their hayloft with that jigger-face Eleazar Ewing!"

"I SAID LOOK FOR SOME NICER STORIES, LULA!"

So Lula Belle says, "Will you get married, Dale?"

"Oh, I reckon. Maggie said we had to go to bed at ten. That's half an hour." Dale puts the Bible back on the shelf over the trunk and reaches a book out from behind and then sits again at the table with it.

"Maggie Jo will be home from Chesley's any time now," says Dale. "You better go on up and get ready for bed." She leafs through the book.

"What's that book you got there?"

"Nothing."

"It's a romance novel!" says Lula Belle, seeing an illustration. "You ain't supposed to be reading those!"

"Oh, ain't I?" snorts Dale. "Don't you tell!" She knows Maggie Jo can't read, and so she feels relatively safe. However, the illustrations, copperplate engravings full of dainty women with round chins and feet the size of pie-wedges, massive dresses and pencil-thin waists, and men with great chests and swords, are a dead giveaway.

"Let me look at it," says Lula Belle, crowding up.

Dale decides the secret is more delicious if it is shared. It becomes a conspiracy.

"Look at these illustrations here! Look at that dress. It's

en feston with alternate flounces and muslin undersleeves. Wouldn't Tom Bodine take a second look at me if I had a dress like that?''

Lula Belle looks carefully: "What's the name of it?''

"The Enemy Conquered, or *Love Triumphant.* 'Her heart yielded to no feeling but the love of Captain Armstrong, on whom she gazed with intense delight.'''

"Read some. Read some more,'' says Lula Belle, for once paying attention to a book.

"I will when you get some sense,'' says Dale, closing the book. "Now we got to go up to sleep.''

Up the narrow stairs, almost a ladder, into the attic, tired and formal in their great flannel nightgowns.

"Goodnight, Dale.''

"Goodnight, Lou.''

"God bless you, Dale.''

"God bless you, Lou.''

At Grandma Maggie Jo's. It is late summer or maybe very early fall and they are making hominy to can for the winter. The corn kernels are being stirred in the big cast-iron pot in a solution of lye and water to slip the hulls. Maggie Joe has put Lula Belle at peeling apples for applesauce. There is a haze all up and down the valley from burning brush-piles, and other kettles in other farmyards.

LULA BELLE

Dale says if we don't get married, we must be old maids in somebody else's kitchen and work for nothing all our lives. Dale says that this is life: we bind ourselves to foolish men, fiddlefoots, gandy-dancers, men who are in love with the racetrack, with the railroad, a jug or a bottle, in love with the last idea they had, the one yesterday, the one the day before; we must entwine our hands beneath the willow and become as one. Gaze on somebody with intense delight. Then you have a home of your own. Right now our dresses is made of cotton domestic and our shoes wouldn't hold walnuts without leaking. From what they all say, this is where our fortune lies—in Love Triumphant *or* The Enemy Conquered.

"Now when you peel them apples, Lula Belle," calls out Maggie Jo, "keep a continual peel falling and it will fall on the ground and compose the initials of the man you marry."

"Wherever you go," Aunt Lizzy calls from the porch, where she too is peeling apples, "count the white horses that you see, and when you have counted forty, the first man you see in a red shirt will be the man you marry. And you can't count any of them twice!"

"Oh, I don't believe that!" laughs Dale over the steaming hominy kettle like a little witch.

"And don't look at the new moon over your left shoulder or you'll be an old maid!" adds Maggie Jo.

"Catch me being an old maid!" says Dale, thinking of Captain Armstrong.

LULA BELLE

I've been gathering a bag of quilt pieces from here, there and yonder, and they each have a story in them because they were what people were wearing when something happened.

The stories are complicated and sometimes secret. But I have to start back at the beginning of the world. Our family all came from Virginia, a beautiful fair land where they fought the English King a long time ago. This was because he was bothering people and he wouldn't let them make whisky.

Dale is fed up with Lula's mooning over apple peels. "Lula, are you going to come on and help here?"

"Lula, are you going to watch that lye water for the hominy or what, girl?"

Lula Belle continues inventing the history of the Thirteen Colonies:

I could have told the English King never to get between a man and his whisky, but nobody ever listens to me. It's a fact of life. They come by generations out of Virginia, through Tennessee and Kentucky, and some got lost on the way and others were et by things. The Kings and the Burnses, the Burnetts and Huffmans and Hanlins and Speeces and Ewings. The Cumberland Presbyterian preachers come after their erring flocks, which was always a-erring and a-erring. And here we are and we marry our fourth cousins and pull our own teeth and make our own whisky and vote Democrat. The men go off to all the wars that's offered. They like the noise. It's the noise that draws them.

"Lula, come over here and stir this corn!" says Dale. "The hulls are slippin and MY ARM'S TIRED!!"

"Well, give me the stir pole," says Lula Belle as she drifts over to the kettle. "I'll just stir and think."

"Don't put that lid on too tight when you're done," says Dale. "It's boilin', it'll blow up."

Lula Belle goes on to the causes of international conflicts:

They like the bullets and the noise. I have pieces of old uniforms I found, Union ones, because all the Huffman's and the King fought for the Union and that caused a lot of trouble around here, because of that. And then my Uncle Samuel D. Burnett went to fight in the Mexican War in 1846 just to get him a new uniform, and by the time they got to St. Louis to join up, the captain said, "Why boy, the war's over. We won." He was so mad he missed it, he got drunk down on the levee and they had to throw him in jail and then send him home on the War Eagle. Old man Laird Burns, he fought at the battle of New Orleans. He still talks about it even though he's nearly ninety, he says, "Ah, my gurrl, there was martial music and the thrillin' report of the cannon, and our shootin' pieces got so hot they blew up in our faces!"

77

And she has walked off and left the lid on too tight, there is the thrillin' report of a small explosion, and now there is a kettle-full of hulled corn all over the yard and in the Devil's Trumpet vine. The big Barred Rocks come dashing for the corn, rolling from side to side and squawking.

"Lula," shouts Dale, "I told you not to put that lid on too tight!"

"There's hominy all over the yard," says Maggie Jo, dropping the apple-butter funnel.

"Oh, those chickens just love it!" laughs Lula Belle.

Maggie Jo takes up a stick and goes after the Barred Rocks. "Girl, I don't know how you're going to make your way in life if you don't learn your work right."

The neighbor women have come to help Maggie Jo and the girls finish the "Kaleidoscope" quilt. It is a ladies sewing circle, later in the fall, after the fruit and corn and beans have been put up, gardens harvested, threshers fed, hogs butchered and lard rendered down, the cotton picked and packed up in sacks for carding into quilt batts, and a thousand other jobs we can hardly think of from this distance in time and culture. Now there is time to sew.

LULA BELLE

When Dale reads of an evening on that romantic novel, you can see her by the new lamp we got; her eyes move back and forth in jerks like quilting needles...

There is a low hum as the women talk and stitch.

LULA BELLE

Stitching up words and sentences. But you can see a quilt pattern all at once, which is important for the roundness of your brain.

Dale and two other women are going over an old quilt, looking at the pieces of dresses, at the stitches, the prairie-point edging.

"Look here at this quilt piece!" says Dale. "This here is from my dress when I was five years old! Mama sewed it for me. I recall I fell into the salt spring in it! We were visiting with that old Jacob Kendall..."

"Oh, look at this piece, this lavender one with the daisies," says Aunt Lizzy. "That was grandma Mary's dress. She was a Lionberger from the Shenandoah. That was the one she tore up for bandages that time, when his guts was all hanging out."

"Where?" asks Maggi Jo. "I can't hardly see good anymore, Lizzy."

"There, grandma," says Dale, pointing.

"You all seen my Virginia quilt?" says Maggie Jo. "The 'Ladies Fan?'"

Lizzy is going to get bored. "I thought it was Tumbling Blocks."

"It's a Ladies Fan or I'm a Chinaman. Go get it for me, Dale."

Lizzy whispers to Aunt Missouri Abigail, "Did you see what I saw?"

Missouri Abigail leans closer. "What?"

Maggie Jo and Dale have been rooting around in the old trunk and have come up with the Ladies Fan. "See that piece?" says Maggie Jo. "That's the old homespun, that was from one of the Lionberger girls' dresses."

"Wasn't there one of them girls got kilt by Indians?" says Lizzy. "Or et by hogs? No...no...it was they drank opium."

Maggie Jo remembers the stories much better. Her deceased husband's mother was a Lionberger. "No, you're thinking of Sally Louisa, she was in love with Thomas Giles Speece, and he up and married her sister, and so she poured coal-oil over herself and set herself afire. Her mother was a Burnett. Or was she a Boulware? Well, they said it was a regular barbecue, I tell you what."

Lizzy turns back to whispering to Missouri Abigail. "Abigail, I saw...an insect of a kind that is unmentionable foraging about in Lula Belle's braids!"

"Well, God have mercy!" whispers Abigail. "And her dresses is too short. She's eleven and her ankles is still showing about up to her knees!"

"Maggie Johanna is just too old to keep them anymore," whispers Lizzy.

And Abigail whispers back, "Well, where they going to go?"

"Dale, let's make some coffee for these folks," says Maggie Jo, putting the quilt away.

Dale hesitates. "Grandma, we're out of coffee."

"Oh Maggie Johanna," says Abigail, looking up from whispering, "I don't care for any. Not for me."

"Oh, me neither!" says Lizzy. "Why it makes me as jumpy as a cat with nine kittens. I don't know which way to run."

Abigail returns quickly to the stories. "Well how come she wanted to marry a Speece so bad? I wouldn't marry a Speece, they're great big terrible villainous people, they're always investing money in peculiar things..."

Lula Belle has drifted away.

I can't get any material from dream figures, or from folks who have passed away and gone to their reward; all I can get is material from people now for my quilt, except for great-aunt Sally Louisa, who left some quilt pieces before she spontaneously combusted.

The ladies have left, and the Kaleidoscope is now basted onto the batt and the backing. Maggie Jo goes to the dark window, looks out into the moonlight, with her hands around her face.

"Girls, is that your daddy I see a-coming down the road?" she says.

Lula Belle's heart leaps wildly, but she stays within her own world.

LULA BELLE

You could see the daylight between the boards and battens of the old Huffman house, and I loved my old grandmother so much I wanted to make her float up high as the turkey-vultures when you see them on the string of the wind like kites.

The deer are slipping back into the harvested gardens to glean.

"Lula!" shouts Dale. "Come a-running'! It's Poppa!"

LULA BELLE

Oh, they have hymns up there in the great churches of clouds. They see this whole earth like a patchwork quilt, the creeks bordering around, Chouteau Creek, Loutre Creek, Bonne Femme Creek, Hess Creek, Hungry Mother Creek and Short Rations Branch. And these are the quilt patterns the earth appears in, the names of our luck, our habits, and our destinies.

> *The Ohio Star*
> *Log Cabin*
> *Cathedral Windows*
> *Ladies Fan*
> *Card Trick*
> *Broken Dishes*
> *Courthouse Steps and*
> *Alabama Belle. There is*
> *The Road To California*
> *Double Irish Chain*
> *Kaleidoscope*
> *Wedding Ring and*
> *The Drunkard's Path.*

"Is he sober, Grandma?" asks Dale, running out to stand beside Maggie Jo.

"If he ain't, I'll take a stick of kindling to him."

LULA BELLE

I would like to see my grandmother fly high like a turkey vulture, riding the updrafts, but you have to learn to work hard in this life. And the hymn that the turkey vultures sing is "Higher Ground."

CHORUS

Lord lift me up, and let me stand
By faith on Heaven's table-land...

Lula Belle hears heavenly voices. She is caught up in her flight and can't come down and maybe fears to come down; after all, Poppa might not be sober and she loves him so much and it might be safer, all told, up in heaven. It's her seventh fit — a lucky number.

William sits by her bed. "Are you waking up, daughter?"

"Poppa?"

"Well, darlin', you shouldn't get yourself so overworked and excited."

"I saw you coming down the road; I guess I got too excited."

"Do you know what day it is?"

"I was in another land from this. I was very high up. I saw where all the creeks go, and the river."

"Do you want some tea with sugar in it?"

"We ain't got no sugar."

"Lula Belle, I brought ten pounds of it," he says, patting her hand. "And oh, just lots of things."

"There's lights around here," says Lula Belle.

"There is? Where, Lou?"

The girls stand uneasily around the kitchen table, where Maggie Jo has called them for a talk.

LULA BELLE

After a while Maggie Jo couldn't keep us, as she was such an old lady and there was nobody there but us to help, with daddy being gone all the time, and me dropping down in a fit from time to time, although I must insist I was peaceful about it. But Grandma couldn't see one way or the other if we was dressed proper in the mornings or stark naiket, or our hair was sticking out like wild men off of Borneo or if we was clean bald or what.

"Well girls, I guess you'd better pack your traps."

"How come, Grandma?" asks Dale.

"Where we going?" asks Lula Belle.

"I guess I'm too old to look after you-all. I can't see to fix your-alls hair. Lizzy come with Chesley and said your-alls hair wasn't fixed right. They said there was things in your hair. I can't see too good anymore, honey."

"But I washed Lula's hair in coal-oil!" says Dale.

"I love you-all. But my hands is begun to shake so bad and I can't see to fix your-alls hair nor dresses. Lizzy is going to make you some pretty dresses."

"But Grandma," says Dale, crying, "Why can't we just stay with them a little while and then come back and look after you?"

Maggie Jo disengages Dale's hands from her sleeve.

"I'm just glad Samuel died before me," she says. "Samuel wasn't capable anymore. I reckon I'll die here sometime before you-all is big enough to come back and do for me. They say you-all have something in your hair but Lizzy won't say what."

Lula Belle whispers fiercely to Dale; "Oh, I do wish Aunt Lizzy would blow it out her drawers!"

Dale whispers back; "Hush up your mouth, or I'll smack you upside the head such a whack..."

"When I hear the train at night now," says Maggie Jo, "I get up and go out looking, because I think somebody's making a noise. Sounds like somebody cryin' for help."

Lula Belle is crying too, looking wildly for a solution. "Can't you go back to Virginia? We could all go back to Virginia."

"I'll go back to Virginia when I die, honey," says Maggie Jo. "Now, when you-all get all your things in those sugar sacks, I want you to take these here dishes with you over to Lizzy and Chesley. These here are Virginia dishes, from the Lionbergers. It's weeping willow pattern. I got just these two pieces left, just these here two. Now, you girls is going to have to walk over there because Chesley's gone off to Boonville for a week with the wagon. It's fifteen mile. Sleep over at Jacob Kendall's house. You pack them dishes careful and Lizzy will have them to pass down to people."

It is nighttime and the girls are walking down the dirt road that runs along the Lamine River, going north. They are carrying their sugar sacks which contain their few articles of clothing, and the *Love Triumphant* book with the newspaper clipping safely stuck in Chapter 24; Maggie Jo will look after the King family Bible for a while. It is too precious to go walking down a dirt road with. They are carrying the two Virginia dishes — a gravy boat and a plate — as an offering to the Burett's, something to bring into the household of value besides two hungry mouths. They have their combs and ribbons and two quilts. They are walking the fifteen miles up valley to Chesley and Lizzy's because there is nobody to take them, or maybe Maggie Jo is too proud to ask; but, after all, they are young and strong. They started early in the morning but they have dawdled, throwing rocks off the Hess Creek bridge and looking into a cave at the foot of the bluffs. It's late. They don't want to sleep over at Jacob Kendall's house. They've always known there is something Bad about Jacob Kendall, even if Maggie Jo doesn't. He lives alone and he's got a big yellow dog and screaming guinea-hens sitting on his yard rails. They will pretend they can't make it by nightfall.

The moon is one-quarter and setting. It has on a night-gown of flannely mist, spangled with stars. Sometimes hard dry leaves fall from the sycamores in the woods alongside them, and drop into the buckbrush with stiff crashes. Maybe they just like wandering along the roads like gypsies, away from society and all its hopeless rules; rules they will never quite be able to obey.

"See, she was talking about going back to Virginia," says Lula Belle. "That's where mama went when she died."

"It was a manner of speaking, Lou."

"They have honeysuckle parties there. Everybody plays the banjo."

"A honeysuckle party?" Dale snorts. "We ain't going to make it to Kendall's tonight, Lou."

"I wonder how she met Grandpa Samuel? They come from Page County, Virginia. I bet she met him underneath the willow. She gazed upon Samuel Huffman with intense delight and they entwined their hands and became as one."

Dale laughs. "How come you to know this?"

Lula Belle pulls something out of her dress pocket. "Look here, this is her handkerchief. She brought it with her from the Shenandoah. I'm going to put it in my quilt. I have to remember everything she said so that we remember. She said she got up when she heard the train at night to help people, and she said they come over the Cumberland Gap with oxes."

"I wish you'd get things right, Lula," says Dale, trudging on.

"But I am! I am! What else have we got in the world but stories? And listen, listen. She said a long time ago our people were old Scotsmen that come to Virginia before there was a United States to get away from the English King because he wouldn't let them pray unless they prayed like heathens. And they come to a town called Luray. And Samuel's father was John, and before him was James, and before him was Ambrose, and before him was Daniel..."

Dale is tired of ancestors. She sees they are coming near the salt springs, and says "Ain't you tired of walking along in the dead of night carrying a bunch of dishes and saying the Begats?"

"...and before him was George, and before him was John, and then two more Johns, and one of them come in 1690 or something."

Dale forges ahead. "Here's the salt springs, Lula, just up ahead."

Lula Belle veers instantly to the Salt Spring Subject and keeps on either inventing or patching bits together. "And you know what? There's a dead Frenchman down there in that salt spring, pickled like a ham! With his French uniform on and his sword and pistol by his side. Yessir. That's the truth."

Dale has heard this too. "No, Lou, they found that old body over near Cobb Springs in 1809 in a cave."

"I tell you what, cross my heart, Dale, he fell down in that salt spring when they was exploring this country, and he reached down to get him a handful of that salty clay and a great perishing SNAKE!! grabbed him by that gold lace on his wrist and kind of snatched him down there and I swear he's there yet..."

They stop by the grassy flat uphill of the salt springs.

"Let's rest," says Dale. "Let's just rest here. There ain't no Frenchman, Lou. We're just going to have to sleep out under that quilt top of yours."

The girls are wrapped up in their quilts, with the book and the Virginia dishes safely wrapped in the dresses inside the sugar sacks. They sleep with their heads on their coats. The stars are winding down towards midnight.

"How come we have to keep going, Dale? How come we can't just lay down here and make Jesus do all the work?"

"It'll be better over at Chesley and Lizzy's, Lou," sighs Dale. "Really it will. Things will get a whole lot better.

They got a wagon, and lath-and-plaster on the walls, and a china cabinet. They got sugar all the time, and Lizzy makes cornbread with milk, is what I heard."

"What about Grandma Maggie Jo?" asks Lula Belle.

"Daddy will come and do for her, and Ewings rents the fields."

Lula Belle thinks a moment and says: "Daddy is sad all the time, like something was bothering his immortal soul."

"Goodnight, Lou."

"Goodnight, Dale."

"God bless you, Lou."

"Dale, what if something comes up in the night and eats us?"

Dale looks up and finds the Big Dipper, a generous cauldron of star-milk. She says, "Mama is looking down on us from heaven."

"No she ain't," says Lula Belle, grimly. "She's gone to Virginia."

Dale groans. "We said God bless you so you have to go to sleep."

Lula Belle closes her eyes and whispers, "Goodnight, Dale."

"Goodnight, Frenchman," giggles Dale.

And long after they have gone to sleep, a spectral voice from the salt spring says, "Goodnight, leetle girls..."

The next evening. Chesley and Lizzy's farm is backed up against the ridge under Rattlesnake Hill (upon which no one has ever seen a rattlesnake, but there are generous amounts of copperheads), a farm with acres of good bottom-lands and a spring and good timber. The house is a small balloon-frame, with a cookstove chimney and no fireplace.

LULA BELLE

Dale says I don't remember when Mama died, but I remember. When she died, she come to me in a dream to say goodbye. She said, Oh how I hate to leave my baby girls. She said, So long, darlings. She said, Bury me beneath the willows. She said, Oh fare thee well, sweetheart, Captain William, I'm off over the mountains, and then she flew away back to the Shenandoah Valley, which is very sweet and very fair. The whippoorwills all go to the Shenandoah in the winter and then come to Missouri every spring. And mama isn't really buried anywhere; you can hear her singing...

CHORUS

I'm going there to see my mother
She said she'd meet me when I come
I'm only going over Jordan
I'm only going over home...

LULA BELLE

You learn that there are people who will take in the stranger at the door and those who will not. You learn to be subtle and sly, judging the quality of the refreshments or the accommodations, you learn to hide.

Chesley escorts the girls upstairs to the attic and says, "Now, Lula Belle and Dale, we're going to put you up here by the chimney and you'll be warm all winter."

"Lula, there ain't no heat up here," says Dale in a fierce whisper.

"Well, we got to put up with it," says Lula Belle.

"We're going to have to sleep upside the chimney to keep warm."

"You take one side and I'll take the other," says Lula.

Later that night, Lizzy and Chesley are talking downstairs in the kitchen. Chesley says, "Elizabeth, you are not charged with admonishing the erring."

"It was fifteen men from around here that took that black man out and hung him," says Lizzy.

Chesley would like sometimes to run out the door and leave the county but says, "Dixie Kendall had a black baby and everybody knew who the father was! It was a known thing that he forced her! That he caught her in the barn and forced his attentions upon her! That outrages were visited upon that woman by a nigger! I want you to ponder that."

"Old man Kendall kept those girls locked up like they was in jail," says Lizzy, keeping at it. "How come their mother ran off? She run off and disappeared and then he chased off every young man that come to call. And so Dixie and the black hired man met in the barn and consorted together. Why, he as good as threw them together! Do you understand what was going on, Chesley? And who's to say they didn't, well, love one another?"

Chesley feels like several of his hairs are turning white as he stands there, one hand on the kitchen pump handle.

"Love one another!! Why, you should talk about cattle and swine loving one another! The Lord God made us separate and we are transgressing his laws when we interbreed, and anyway, I had nothing to do with it!"

Lizzy picks up something from the woodbox she has been keeping for years, and why she has chosen this moment, nobody knows but her. "Then what's this shirt here, Chesley? This blue shirt that was in the barn all those years, smelling like sweat and dying? Why'd you bring it home and keep it, if you didn't want me to ask? And who else was there?"

91

Dale is rigidly awake and the quarter-moon shines in at the dormer window. It is hours later. Dale sits up as she feels Lula come back to bed.

"Lula, you was at the head of the stairs listening."

"Yes."

"What's that you got?"

Lula Belle holds something up to the weak moonlight. "A piece of that black man's shirt. They went to bed and I went down and snuck it."

"You're going to put that in your quilt."

"Jesus knows even when a sparrow falls," says Lula Belle. "Though it don't do the sparrow no good. And fifteen men went and took that black man out and hung him."

Dale had the piece of cloth in her hand — she drops it. "That's a black man's! And he went and died in it! It's prolly got cooties!"

"So did we," says Lula Belle..."Dale, do you think Daddy might have been one of those men?"

"Oh never! He'd never!" says Dale in an angry whisper as she thrashes around in the covers. "Sometimes he don't know what he's doing when he's drinking, but he don't ever fight. He just gets drunk and falls down."

"Yes, he don't ever fight," agrees Lula Belle, relieved.

"What a terrible story, Lou. Did Dixie Kendall really have a black baby?"

"That's what they say. But I don't know, I never seen her, she went to Illinois. Lizzy said old man Kendall kept the two of them locked in the barn all day and all night so that they consorted together. Is it consorting that gives you a baby?"

"I think so."

"Is consorting a word like drawers? You ain't supposed to say drawers."

"No," decides Dale, "you can say consort."

"It will be the thing to keep him in remembrance," says Lula Belle, full of the sense of power that storytellers are often charged with. "If ever that baby grows up, I'll say to it someday, see this here piece of blue workshirt, in my Wedding Ring quilt? This was your daddy that they hung."

Dale likes this thought. "It will be the consorting piece."

"Yes, the consorting piece."

"Goodnight, Lou."

"Goodnight, Dale."

"God bless you, Lou."

"God bless you, Dale."

Lula Belle sits on the rails of the salt spring communing with the Frenchman. He is wearing knee britches, his sword and pistol by his side.

LULA BELLE

One night I got very lonesome for my father, for him to protect me against the world and all its snares and traps, that I walked away from the Burnetts one night to go down to the railroad tracks to see if I could see him coming by.

93

She can hear a whistle in the distance.
The Frenchman leads the chorus:

> *Someone's in the kitchen with Dinah*
> *Someone's in the kitchen I know*
> *Strumming on the old banjo*
> *and that's just how it goes, you know?*
> *It was astonishing, it was amusing.*

LULA BELLE

They said I'd taken a fit. And so here we are. But I know Daddy wants us to grow up in a home with lath-and-plaster on the walls and a china cabinet. He worked all up and down the Katy line, swinging his red bull's eye lantern in the night, to tell the trains how to keep on the tracks, and with his big long face and the light shining up, it looks like he's saying:

THIS WAY TO HELL!

He'll go off some night like a shooting star and end up in Oklahoma. He needs somebody to take care of him, that's what it is.

At William Nelson's house near Otterville. This is the house he inherited from his father, and where the family had lived before Nanni died. It has a second story added on to a large log cabin and then sided over. He stays there when he is not travelling as a brakeman. He is a bachelor without comforts, except for old man Hanlin's whisky.

"William Nelson, I heard you were to home," says Lucifer.

LULA BELLE

That's why me and Dale can't go live with him, really. Because you ever know when Lucifer comes to visit him and he and the devil have to have a drink together.

"How did you come to know that?" says William.

"Why, I stopped at Lost Corners to inquire for you and the man who keeps that dissolute and sordid whisky-shop told me you would be at home looking after your hangover. He said you were very merry, he said you had retired quite late."

"Well, the horse brought me home, I guess."

Lucifer's statements leak flaming into the room. He wears knee britches and gold lace, and he has a sword and pistol by his side. "We should have a drink together to keep off the delirium tremens."

"I wasn't planning on having any delirium tremens," says William.

"Of course you are. I am them," says Lucifer.

William remembers something practical he ought to do. "I was going into Otterville to get my hair cut."

"You couldn't even get them harness buckles done up, if you were going to take the buggy. Got anything in the pie safe, here? Or, if you were going to ride, I doubt if you could catch that contrary horse of yours."

"I think I have an allergy to whisky, you know. I should never drink it," says William, as he watches Lucifer rummage around in the pie safe. "I'm a Cumberland Presbyterian, you know."

"I have more Cumberland Presbyterians down in hellfire than any other denomination, I assure you. It's because everything going is a sin for a Presbyterian. I didn't invent sin, you know. People make up sin for themselves. If they say card-playing and cosmetics is sinful, why, I am amiable, come on down to the Lakes Of Fire! I have no objections. And then they pass over in silence the times they took out and hung people down in the draw of Chouteau Creek in the dead of night. Ah, here's that whisky."

"I had nothing to do with taking out and hanging people!" says William, jumping up. "Nothing at all in this world."

"And if you didn't, could you have stopped it? Saying here, or allowing, just for the conversation, that you didn't"

"I said I was going into town to get my hair cut, and I'm going if I never cock another gun."

"Have one first," says Lucifer, pouring out two glasses of brimstone and sulphur. "Where's them two girls of yours?"

"They've gone to live with relatives up in Buffalo Prairie. I couldn't keep them after their mother died."

Lucifer nods. "You couldn't take care of them before, either."

"No sir, not in the least is that the truth! It was after their mother died that I took to drinking. After the funeral I drank so much I wasn't fit to be with for two weeks. I ended up in a house next to Lost Corners. I don't recall how I got there. But I know how I left — laying in a democrat."

"It is said there are disreputable women in that house,"
says Lucifer, drinking up his own glass. "A woman who
drinks opium, and another who tells fortunes with cards
and a crystal ball — the sort of women no gentleman
would speak their name in the family abode."

"We didn't have no family abode by that time."

"Your oldest daughter is coming of age," says Lucifer.
"She's been visiting over at Bodine's farm. There is a
young man there as you might know. Tom Bodine is now
twenty-one. He's broken a hundred acres of upland all
his own. And when Old Man Bodine dies — my goodness,
dear fellow! All that bottomland!"

"Visiting Tom Bodine?" shouts William. "Over my dead
body! Over my dead body she'll go walking disorderly
about this valley with some young buck that don't know
how to keep his pecker in his pants!"

"And Lula Belle is fourteen," says Lucifer. "You've been
careless and indifferent about their soul's best interests.
You must see to the cultivation of their Christian characters."

"I'm going to get you drunk, sir," says William, jumping
up. "And then I'm going to set this house on fire and burn
you down with it."

"This house is already on fire," agrees Lucifer. "I already
burnt down with it. I fell out of the bottom end of heaven
and burnt my wings. I am life's other side. I am the Son
of the Morning when the darkest hour is just before dawn,
and I came with you all out of Virginia. I've burnt down
your houses many times."

William Nelson King takes the bottle from Lucifer and
throws it into the woodstove, and the lamp turns over and
the oil runs and the pie safe catches fire and everything
catches fire.

"All you Speeces were great big villainous people," says William.

At Chesley and Lizzy's farm under Rattlesnake Hill. Dale sits in a rocking chair. She looks across the Burnett bottomland to the line of trees along the Lamine River, the bluffs and chimney rock on the other side, at the turkey vultures riding the updrafts. Lula Belle comes out.

"Dale, what are you doing sitting out here on the porch?"

"Nothing."

"You're reading that book."

"What of it?" says Dale, shutting the book. "Go away and give me some peace."

"Dale, what if we never did get married? When you're married you can't own anything; Uncle Chesley told me your husband owns everything."

Dale clutches *Love Triumphant.* "I said go away, Lula, and give me some peace."

Lula Belle walks down the front porch steps toward the pear tree. "Well, alright then."

Dale takes up the book and reads: "'Her lofty beauty, seen by the glimmering of the chandelier, filled his heart with rapture. 'Lady Ambulinia,' said he, trembling, "I have long desired a moment like this. I dare not let it escape.' Lady Ambulinia's countenance showed uncommon vivacity, with a resolute spirit. 'Captain Armstrong,' said she... " Dale shuts the book. "Well, I'll just run off with him then, if Poppa won't let me get married."

Chesley is in the buggy, pulling up to the train station in Otterville. He ties the horses and walks in, up to the telegraph operator in the operations room.

"Here, you," says Chesley, leaning across the counter, "I want you to send this to William Nelson King at the roundhouse in Jefferson City. He's a brakeman on the Katy."

The operator doesn't know Chesley, but he knows William. "You bet."

"Send this. 'Your eldest daughter about to run off with Tom Bodine, return Otterville next train, suggest marriage be planned this spring. Girls to move to Abigail and Henry T.'s.'"

The operator happily takes the paper out of Chesley's hand. "Why, that scoundrel," he says.

"Who?"

"Tom Bodine."

Chesley waits for the gravity of the situation to sink in. "I don't feel you should concern yourslef with this, and if you do, you'll soon be wearing that instrument around you neck. Now send that."

"Yes, sir."

We are at the graveyard across from New Lebanon Church, near the big pine.

LULA BELLE

They said the best sermon over Maggie Jo. It was March, and there was a rainstorm. Her whole name was Margaret Johanna Burnett Huffman, she was nearly eighty-nine years old. She taught me to work hard in life, and how to get along without no sugar and how to make hominy corn and about salt and spiders and the new moon. She taught me how to endure what is hard in life. She taught me all the quilt patterns there ever was. And her own pattern was the Ladies Fan, because she always kept the air a-stirring around her, and her mind was very fanciful. Dale was all tore up because Grandma wouldn't get to see her wedding this June, and she cried into her hands all during the funeral, it sounded like a train, it sounded like somebody crying for help.

The Chorus is made up of many ancestors buried here, there, yonder, and in Virginia.

And in the final days, the clouds openeth and the grandmothers rain down upon us.

"Oh, Lula," whispers Dale, "nobody said that!"

CHORUS

Yea, it is said, children and fools speak the truth and this seems to mean that wise people and grownups prevaricate.

Yes, the secrets and the lies are manifold; many are called by grace, but few answer, and if they do, they give the wrong name.

"Oh, Lula," snuffles Dale, "if you're going to repeat the sermon, do get it straight!"

CHORUS

Cross the Lamine River, the Blackwater River, cross thou Hess Creek, Loutre Creek, Chouteau Creek, Hungry Mother Creek and Short Rations Branch, walk even beyond the salt springs, which welleth up like the bullets of desperadoes and the tears of the dispossessed, the young fresh tears of motherless children.

A solo voice sings "The Darkest Hour Is Just Before Dawn" or "Life's Other Side."

CHORUS

Fear not! Thy grandmothers shall give thee Virginia dishes of the best willowware, and thou shalt break them. Thy grandmother shall give thee all the tall jewelry of the Shenandoah, and thou shalt lose it, but the quilts thou shalt lose not.

"Lou, you just hear what you want to hear," says Dale. "You make it up. Now don't cry. They're going to shovel in the dirt."

CHORUS

The quilts break not and they are too big to fall down cracks. Thy grandmothers are sending thee into the next century with rags and the design of rags and these shall defend thee against all manner of ee-vell.

"Oh, Lou!" says Dale, beginning to quietly shake with laughter.

CHORUS

Of the rags and tatters of the poor, the humble, the dispossessed and the hanged one, thou shalt make quilts, and these will tell their stories time without end, and protect thee with stories, even though the earth shall burn and the heavens be rolled up like a scroll. Amen!

In Aunt Missouri Abigail's Kitchen. The girls are now living with Aunt Missouri Abigail and Uncle Henry T.

LULA BELLE

After awhile Chesley and Lizzy said we had to go live with Aunt Missouri Abigail and Uncle Henry T., because Chesley didn't want to be responsible in case Dale ran off with Tom Bodine, and we was so contrary. So we packed our things, the quilts and the Virginia dishes, as we decided not to let Lizzy have them, and we moved again. Dale said it was all a trouble and a trial, but she would soon be married and have a home of her own.

The girls are washing dishes. They have taken out the two Virginia pieces as well; the willow patterns are dusty.

"How do you fortell the future, Dale? Can you go to a witch-woman?"

"I reckon...There's an astrologer, like a kind of fortune-telling woman at the county fair."

Lula Belle squashes lye soap into the washpan. "Maybe it's sinful," she says. "Like when King Saul called up the Witch of Endor to see what the dead people were doing down there."

"Well," says Dale, "her name is Madame Perrigo, but just don't let anybody find out. Especially Aunt Missouri Abigail her very own self, alright?"

Lula Belle is happy with this answer, and starts singing: "Frog went a-courtin' and he did ride..."

"A rig-dom-bottom-mitch-i kimbo!"

"A sword and pistol by his side..." sings Lula Belle.

A rig-dom-bottom-mitch-i kimbo!

Keemo-kimo, haro-jaro, hey catch a rat trap pennywinkle flammadoodle,

A-rig-dom-bottom-mitchi-i kimbo!

Lula is jumping to the singing and drops a dish.

"Oh, Dale! Grandma's dish!!"

"That was Grandma's *Virginia* dish!"

"I killed it," says Lula Belle, holding up the blue-willow pieces.

"I ain't never seen such a dead dish," says Dale, as she starts sweeping it up. They start to giggle.

"I went and broke my grandma's dish..." sings Lula.

And Dale joins in: *A rig-dom-bottom-mitchi-i kimbo!*

"And I really do not give a piss..." contributes Dale.

"So hang me for a Methodist!" says Lula Belle.

Keemo-kimo, haro-jaro, hey catch a rat trap pennywinkle flammadoodle, a rig-dom-bottom-mitchi-i kimbo!

They toss up the broken pieces.

"My daddy's house went and burnt down..." adds Lula.

"And now he's living in a tavern in the town!" sings Dale.

They are becoming hysterical with laughter.

"He'd drink more liquor but he can't get it down!" adds Lula Belle.

Keemo-kimo, haro-jaro, hey catch a rat trap pennywinkle flammadoodle, yellowbug, a rig-dom-bottom-mitchi-i kimbo!

Dale listens a moment, and then cries, "Oh, no, Aunt Abigail's coming! She heard us! I'm leaving!" and flees the scene. As she runs, she bumps into the kitchen table; a crash.

"Godalmighty, Dale!! You went and broke the *other* one!" cries Lula Belle, holding the fragments.

Aunt Abigail sails into the room, redheaded and full of power. "*What* did I hear you say, Lula Belle King?"

"I said piss and I said Godalmighty," says Lula Belle, and stares back at her.

"There are words I will not allow to be said in my house and you say them at your peril. I will put you and your sister out on the road. You will go to the poorhouse."

"My daddy will come and get us!"

"That desperate and intemperate drunkard will never come and get anybody. I want an apology."

"I'm sorry, Aunt Abigail," says Lula Belle, giving in.

"Well, there are some things that just cannot be apologized for. You think you can use language like that in my house and then just apologize..."

Lula Belle starts backing out of the kitchen.

"...and then everything's alright; well, you can think twice, sister..."

The only response to Aunt Missouri Abigail's self-righteous superiority is flight. Lula Belle runs out of the house, past the pear tree, and pauses by the washhouse.

"Dale! Are you back here?"

"I'm in the woodshed," whispers Dale.

The woodshed is musty and spidery; it smells like cedar and lye. They clang into froes and saws.

"What're we going to do?" says Lula Belle.

"I don't *know*. I don't *want* to live with relatives no more. I'm too big! Too big to be hollered at like that. And I ain't got no stockings, even."

"She made me apologize and then she said..."

"I know. She always does that. She makes people apologize and then says an apology ain't good enough. Thank God I'm going to be married. Nobody will fool with me then."

"I'm going to put a piece of her *drawers* in my quilt and say to everybody, that was from my Aunt Missouri Abigail, the HORSE'S ASS!!" says Lula Belle.

"Drawers! Drawers!" laughs Dale.

"Piss! Testicles! Organs!" shouts Lula Belle, becoming intemperate.

"Damn! Hell! Male Organs!!" cries Dale.

"Female organs!! Buttocks!"

"Penises! Shit! Damnation and Faust!!" shouts Dale.

And then they sing, together and in harmony:

And it was from Aunt Dinah's quilting party,
he was seeing Nellie home...

At Aunt Abigail and Henry T.'s place. It is Dale's wedding. The yard is full of wagons and the women have been pressing dresses and crinolines for days with the old sad irons, family silver has come out of the silver cases, and cream for the whipping is being kept cool in the spring-house. Aunt Missouri Abigail has baked three layers of cake in her new "Prosperous" cookstove, and Uncle Henry T. has brought ice from Otterville, packed in saw-dust in the wagon. All of these efforts say they are sorry they made Dale go without stockings and do all the hand-mangling jobs like shelling field corn — but now they will be rid of their obligation. Her husband will buy her stockings. She will be "married off," and this shows they are generous people after all, aren't they? Dale and Thomas Sheridan Bodine have been through the marriage cere-mony at the church, made promises to the community and God and each other, and have returned to Aunt Abigail's and Henry T.'s for the wedding party.

LULA BELLE

A week before Dale's wedding I had come down with a fainting fit again, and had called out the names of lost and departed ones, and I was visited by the Frenchman who lives in the salt springs, who was very well-connected, he said, in the other world, and for a week after I saw lights around things, and so it was lovely and amusing at Dale's wedding, and there were so many lamps. I bet it was like that in Virginia, I reckon they had beautiful dresses, and gentlemen, and a hundred fiddlers at every wedding...

Dale and Lula Belle, aunts, cousins and friends are in the back room getting themselves ready. Dale's dress is a vast green and lavender plaid taffeta.

"Oh, Dale, it's very fetching and smart," says Caledonia.

"Daddy brought me the taffeta. It's en feston with alternate flounces."

"Dale, you're so young, honey," says Lizzy. "Now don't go wading in the creek with it."

"Oh, I thought I'd go slop Chesley's hogs with it," says Dale. "Them hogs have made it to every funeral and wedding that I know of."

"Well, they're here all right," says Lizzy. "On a plate. Maybe you want some lemons and salt, Dale, you look faint."

Dale is putting tiny white bloodroot flowers in her corona of braids. "Oh, I'm alright," says Dale. "Give me that fan there, that Jesus fan. Well, at least he ain't a Baptist."

"Who are you referring to?" sniffs Aunt Abigail. "Jesus?"

The other women burst out laughing.

"I fail to see what's funny," says Abigail, sternly.

Two women cousins fall to snorting. "She fails to see...!" And then the fiddle starts up "Here Come The Bride!"

"This is you, Dale, go on," says Lizzy.

There is a tearing sound as Dale tears a flounce off her dress.

"Lula Belle, here's a piece of my wedding dress to put in that quilt of yours, darlin'."

"Dale!! You tore a flounce of your dress!"

"And you tell the story of how I nearly had to run off with Tom Bodine before Daddy would take any notice at all," says Dale, kissing Lula on the cheek. "Is that a big enough piece?"

"I will treasure it with all my heart and put it right in the middle," says Lula Belle, stashing it in the sleeve of her new dress.

Applause as Dale enters the living room. The furniture has all been moved to the barn to make room for the dance.

Thomas Sheridan, stiff in a five-button cutaway, turns to Dale. "Mrs. Bodine, I thought you were going to keep me waiting forever."

"Ladies and gentlemen, form up for the Virginia Reel," calls out the fiddler, a big villainous Speece. "Just form up there; you all going to dance or what?"

"I'll have the first dance with my daughter, Mr. Bodine," says William.

A man in the crowd whispers loudly: "He's gone and bought a pony keg of whisky and I'll be goddamned if he didn't drink the greater part of it himself...excuse my language."

"Mr. King, remove yourself from the dance," says the fiddler. "You're a bit too merry."

"Shut your mouth, George Speece!" says William. "Son of a bitch, fifteen years ago it would have been as much as your life was worth..."

"Mr. King," insists the fiddler, "leave the premises."

"Oh, poppa, please..." pleads Dale.

"To tell me to remove *my* premises! You Confederate son-of-a-bitch!" shouts William.

"William!"

"Mr. King!"

"How'd I miss you at Wilson's Creek is what I want to know!" says William, suddenly possessed by memories of the battle of Wilson's Creek, with him on one side and the Speece brothers on the other. "I should have blowed your head off when it was legal!"

"I will remove you myself, then!" yells the fiddler.

"Well, who's a-henderin' you?" says William, as he takes off his coat.

Lula Belle runs out and grabs his arm. "Daddy, dance with me."

"Get out of here, Lula. Go on. Go away. Daddy wants to fight."

The fiddler thinks better of it and begins playing instead. The guitar and mandolin follow.

"Dance with Lula, Daddy, and come on now..." says Dale, as she joins her sister.

Outside at night: guests are leaving, wagons creak off, people have had a good time anyway. That's what they came for, by God.

"Well, sister," says Dale, and leans out of the wagon, "we'll be off now."

The two of them hold hands.

"Soon as we get back from Jeff City you'll come and visit, Lula," says Tom. "Don't worry! You'll come and stay with us! Now, where's your dad?"

"I put him to sleep in the upstairs," says Lula. Well..."

"Goodnight, Dale."

"Goodnight, Lou."

"God bless you, Dale."

"God bless you, Lou."

Lula Belle and her father are crossing the valley by wagon. Lula Belle is moving back to Lizzy and Chesley's again. Now, instead of a sugar sack she has a small carpet bag, and a few things left to her by Maggie Jo. She has the King Family Bible with the clipping in it.

LULA BELLE

The last time I moved anyplace was back again with Uncle Chesley and Aunt Lizzy, because me and Aunt Missouri Abigail couldn't stand each other. And my daddy took me over there in the wagon. We come down the long road through the valley.

And as they ride along, they silently note who is planting what, and how the small patches of cotton are growing, and the wheat. The sun is shining on Chimney Rock and on the ridges around them.

LULA BELLE

We came down the long road through the valley, at evening, through Buffalo Prairie, in September, and the moon was coming up on one side of the world and the sun was going down on the other. And turkey buzzards were uplifting on the air drafts like ashes flying in the heat of the sunset fire, and I think one of them was carrying the soul of my grandmother on his back. The road was still hot from the day, but the air was cool, and it made a heavy mist in the valley of the Lamine River and the hollows of the creeks, liquid and white, Chouteau Creek and Loutre Creek, Hess Creek and Hungry Mother Creek and Short Rations branch. And daddy took the opportunity to tell me he was quitting the railroad and going out west to the Indian Nation. He said that railroad men tempted him to drink and his oldest daughter was married and gone, and there was only me to be married yet. So he might as well go on out and drive a combine team in the harvest season. There were Cherokees out there, he said, and Chickasaws, and Wyandottes. And oh, how the fields of the valley did shine along beside us, it was rich and very blue, with the heads of sorghum sticking up like soldier's plumes, and every hollow filled with our people and all our stories, the good and the bad of them all, places where people had a good time and places where they died. Driving past all these stories was like running a stick down a picket fence in your mind. And so me and Daddy talked at last and said all that was in our hearts. Well, that's not altogether true. Dale says I have to be more rigorous with myself about reporting conversations. I guess I asked him about his life and he told me. That's how it was, yes, I'm sure that's pretty well accurate.

"Well, poppa, did you ever kill a man?"

"I did," says William, after a long thought.

"When did you do that?"

William sighs and looks out over Jacob Kendall's fields. "I wish I had a son I could tell this to."

"I was just asking," says Lula Belle, and pulls up her tapestry shawl, her good one.

"Well, it was in the War."

"What happened?"

"It was at Lexington; the Battle of Lexington up there on the Missouri River. The Confederates come over the breastworks — they were cotton bales we'd pitched up — and we were out of ammunition, you see, and hadn't had a drink of water in two days; we were dying of thirst — and then they set fire to the cotton bales. There was many a man died there in the smoke of it....And they made a charge, and a fellow come over the top of them cotton bales and since I didn't have any bullets I stuck the ramrod down the barrel of my musket and poured in a load of black powder and shot him through the breast. Transfixed him. I'm sorry I did it. He was a young fellow. So was I. I was a young fellow too. We hadn't any water for so many days....I saw men drinking the bloody water the surgeons was going to throw out. I guess I cultivated a permanent thirst, there. Been thirsty ever since then."

"Who was it?" asks Lula Belle.

"Who was what?" says William, looking at her.

"The fellow you transfixed."

"Why, I don't know," says William, shaking his head. "He wasn't from around here. I think he was with a Tennessee Regiment."

"Who was you with?"

"The 49th Missouri Volunteers, Company C. Now, let's not talk about the War ever again. Most of your uncles went to the Confederacy and we must cease any discussion of it from this time forth."

"Yes, daddy. But you know, I can't rest until I know something."

"What?" sighs William.

"Well, that black man they took out and hung, was that 'Jim Drew, Worthless Otterville Negro?' "

"Well, I'll be goddamned," says William, muttering to himself. "Lulu, the things you get your mind around... well, I guess you can't help it.... Yes. But listen. He wasn't worthless. No man is worthless. God accepts everybody, and I ought to know. Believe me, I ought to know. Now hush up about it."

"Daddy..."

"What, darlin'?"

"Where you going this time?"

"To Oklahoma, to the Indian Nation."

"How come?"

"Well, daughter, if I go out there and work in the hay-fields, there's not...they don't have any whisky out there, on account of the Indians. So there won't be any for me to be tempted by. And then...well, I'll be making a lot of money, you know. I'm good with a team. And I'll send you taffeta silk for your wedding dress, and...what else would you want?"

"What else would I want? Well, I really don't know..."

"Well..." laughs Lula Belle.

William is happy to get away from war and murder and onto beaux. He doesn't want to make the same mistake he did with Dale.

"You can tell your daddy."

"No, poppa, really I don't have any in mind. But... send me the silk taffeta *anyway*."

"It's a promise, Lula."

Going to the Cooper County Fair. The Burnetts will take her now that there is only one of them. It's a long trip: nearly thirty miles and they will stay overnight.

LULA BELLE

And so I went to the Cooper County Fair in Boonville, with Aunt Lizzy and Uncle Chesley, and I took with me the anxieties and fears that I held in my heart. For I didn't know what was to become of me in the world, and I didn't know what to do with myself. And so I decided to go to Madame Perrigo with a dollar that daddy had sent me from the Indian Nation.

South of the fairgrounds the wagons are parked, with awnings stretched from the wagonboxes to poles, and under the awnings quilts and straw mattresses are laid out. The men are in knots talking carefully about their cattle. Sometimes women, too, have hogs or sheep or cattle to sell and so they stand at the edge of these discussions. This is the local economy of Cooper County. It is dominated by white men who are Baptists, vote Democrat and have pianos in their parlours. Lizzy is entering a lace tablecloth and Grandma Maggie Jo's Kaleidoscope quilt. Altho Lizzy has finished the quilt herself, she wants to enter it under Maggie Jo's name. She is worried about whether this will be allowed or not. Chesley has brought nothing to show but he might buy; he heads directly toward a group of men he knows who are dealing in the new Herefords. They said there was to be a Hereford bull at the fair.

LULA BELLE

There were so many things at the Cooper County Fair! People that had a lot of hair, and a woman with a mustache, and vegetables being judged for moisture and tint, animals and their progeny, a boar pig the size of a woodshed, it was tumultuous, it was amusing. You could eat cotton candy and lose your entire face in it, they had fetching little kewpie dolls as adorable as candy hearts, and the horses that came to show! I never expect to sit on a horse like that, and Aunt Lizzy said...

"Well, Lula, maybe you'll marry a man that likes horses," says Lizzy as she bustles along to the Home Arts building, grasping the quilt and the lace tablecloth.

Lula Belle talks Lizzy into letting her go by herself to the Poultry building, but instead heads for the Midway.

LULA BELLE

And so I took my dollar and I went to see the fortune teller, Madame Perrigo, as soon as I could cut loose from Lizzy and Chesley.

"She reveals secrets no mortal ever knew!" says the barker. "She restores happiness to those who, from doleful events, catastrophes, crosses in love, loss of relatives, money or friends, have become despondent! Gives you the name, likeness, and characteristics of the one you will marry! From the stars we see in the firmament, she deducts the future destiny of man! Go in through there, young lady.

"Thank you, sir," says Lula Belle, and walks into the sinfully brilliant calico curtains, into a place whose decorations and furnishings scream "Mystery!!" instead of "Propriety." It is lit by a coal-oil lamp and there is a small crystal ball.

Madame Perrigo is satisfyingly gypsy: scarves, rings,

deep eyes and rouge and an accent.

"Well, you're only about as big as a minute, honey. I don't know if you're big enough to have a future yet. Save yourself a dollar and wait a few years."

"I'm fourteen," says Lula Belle. "And I have two very important questions."

"Of course," nods Madame Perrigo and shuffles her cards. "Of course."

LULA BELLE

Oh, she was beautiful. She had fringes and crystal shade weights hanging off all over her, she had a deck of cards that was all pictures, and earrings on either side of her head that looked like advertisements for ears. Her hair was unnaturally black and she had a voice that reached backwards into time and forwards into the future.

"Now, here are the cards laid out. And what are your questions?"

"One question is, who will I marry, and the other is of great import."

"Aha. One has to meditate and empty one's mind of any knowledge connected to the subject....Now, I will read. In the position of your past, I see a boneyard. You got two dead people back there."

"One of them was my mother when I was little."

Madame Perrigo nods in agreement. "The cards never lie," she says. "Now, in your immediate future, I see a journey where you will meet your intended. Probably a long voyage into the next county."

"Oh, I would like that!"

"And here in your house of family and relations, there are absent ones."

"Yes," says Lula Belle. "You see, my momma died when I was young and then my daddy had to go away to work in the Indian Nation. And also I had brain fever when my momma died so I have visions."

Perrigo looks up, suddenly cautious, and her earrings flash. "You have *visions?*"

"Yes," says Lula Belle. "Now, do I *have* to get married?"

Perrigo stares at her, wondering if the girl is pregnant. "Do you have to...well, what else are you going to do? And you with visions!"

"I don't know. I can't read or write at all. Look there — what's that card?"

"That's Temperance," says Perrigo, looking down. This isn't going right; this fourteen-year-old has taken over the reading.

"Read that card," says Lula Belle.

"Well, Temperance is a good card, balance and harmony. You see there, she's pouring something out of a jug. That's in your house of distant future."

"That's my daddy."

"He knocks back a few, does your daddy?"

"He's trying *not* to."

"Good for your daddy," says Perrigo. And this here..."

"It's the hanged man!!" says Lula Belle, jumping up. "That's what I wanted to ask you about!"

"...this here is about your future intended," says Perrigo, quickly shifting the subject. "You'll get married all right."

"Well, what about you, have you been married?"

"Repeatedly."

"Maybe I could tell fortunes?" asks Lula Belle.

"Honey," says Perrigo, shaking her head, "they'd run you out of whatever church you go to on Sunday and, besides, it's an occult art. Now settle down and listen here to this about your intended."

"No, no, I want to hear about the Hanged Man. That was my other question. There was a man, a black man that they took out and hung on November 29th, 1876, down by the draw of Chouteau Creek, and I want to know if my daddy, who is William Nelson King and who is at present residing in the Indian Territory at no fixed address, if he was in on it, when that man perished, and I can't go on with life until I know."

"My dear!! The cards don't tell that kind of thing! Ain't that a matter for the sheriff?"

"It was seven years ago," says Lula Belle.

Madame Perrigo decides to take it because her knowledge of the incident is secular and not divine.

"I see. November 29th, 1876. William Nelson King. Yes. Bill King."

"Do you know him?" asks Lula Belle.

"Well, in a way."

"Then what does the Hanged Man say?"

"Alright. Though it may be perilous to enquire of matters that are occult and dark, and in the past, I shall enquire. Spirits, come! Speak! Ahhhh.... Indeed, the card says your daddy on the night in question was disporting himself in a house in Lost Corners and he was so merry he was incapacitated and couldn't have hung anybody if he tried. Now that information is tendered you in secret and if you ever reveal it your daddy will have your hide, and life would become somewhat uncomfortable for me. Don't you ever tell him you come to see Madame Perrigo, my dear."

"Cross my heart and hope to die, stick a thousand

needles in my eye."

"Good, good. Whew. Now, for your intended...you'll marry a Baptist."

"What!! " says Lula Belle, shoving the cards away. "I ain't going to marry no Baptist!"

"That's the breaks, kid. And you will have a hard life."

"I *already* had a hard life," says Lula Belle.

"You'll have *more* hard life," says Perrigo, gathering up the cards. "Ah...you are doing something in secret, are you not?"

"Yes...yes, I'm making a quilt with patches from everybody's clothes in them, to remember the stories that are told, and what happened to people."

"Ah," says Perrigo, smiling a little doubtfully, "that's lovely."

"And they're just like your cards there. I mean, there's the Hanged Man, and there's Temperance with her jug, and people falling from the burning tower, that's when my daddy fought at Lexington, and what's this one, the man stepping out over the cliff, with the dog and the rose?"

"That's the Fool card, honey. He's going to step out over that cliff and *fly.*"

"Then that's my grandma, Maggie Jo!"

"Well," says Perrigo, returning to the reading, "here's the final outcome. Yes...hmmm...your life will be hard but your quilts will become a precious heirloom, and none of your stories will ever be forgotten, because they are so fetching and so strange. It'll be just like one of them romance novels, where, you know, where people cry over the last pages, and sigh to themselves, and just can't put it down, and wish it would start again."

"I know what you mean. Love Triumphant, or The

Enemy Conquered.

"That is very so. Your daddy is a very good looking man, girl, and he's been through the midnight fire, and he means the best for you. Now run along, run along, your cards have been told."

"Thank you, Madame Perrigo! Thank you. Goodbye."

LULA BELLE

The mouth is the place that thoughts leap out of, it is the starting-gate of our hearts. The words of preachers, whispered conversations, stories told sitting on the rails of the salt spring, newspaper talk, the words of fortune tellers. I never looked at the new moon over my left shoulder, and he was the first man I saw after I counted forty white horses. Daddy sent me a dress length of silk taffeta in pale green that he bought in St. Louis, and he is coming home any day now from the Indian Nation. He no longer goes walking disorderly about the county with Lucifer because Lucifer can't locate him. I won't get my quilt finished in time for my wedding, and it won't be finished for years. It is something to amuse myself with, it will be something to give my children. And, oh, one story I forgot was the rose baby that Grandma Huffman saved when she was a midwife, and you know something else? I forgot to tell about how Sylvania Speece and the Hanlin girl sold all Old Man Hanlin's hogs at the fair when he was drunk and run off with the money to...

MONEY AND BLANKETS

RITA JEAN

I get up. I go outside in my mind and leave that hard daily part of me there in bed as a kind of substitute. I wait for the sun to come up. It's the ballast of the underside of the world, that's what makes us so heavy at night in our sleep, except when we can't sleep. Except when all night, all the hot night, the hours have been walking by in hard shoes.

The night proceeds through the clock; stars turn.

"Rita Jean, aren't you asleep yet?" says Harlan, rolling over.

And right at dawn when the light breaks through the hills, it seems like the sun is a city full of people rejoicing, the City of Zion, and you don't need to believe in anything, or study on the right and wrong of everything, but the world will do all the believing for you.

Deer fold themselves up in the deep ravine of the Little Blue Spring River, and cooks and waitresses shut off their alarms.

That's when I go to the creek down by the spring to look for arrowheads, and sometimes they lay there like pointers on a map, left from old wars and deer kills, and it seems important to go the right way, and I'm thinking, where is it? Which way? But it's a map so ancient it was here long before us. And maybe the map has just been lost forever.

The radio alarm goes off, and an announcer cries out: "Good morning from the heart of the Ozarks, Radio KHIK, with country-western hits, it's 6 a.m. and folks, I hate to tell you this, but it's ninety degrees!''

This is where I live, with husband and kid, on my daddy's farm, where we are living rent-free. My name is Rita Jean Stoddard and I'm here to tell you the truth about my life. I might as well, nobody else will.

The morning expands; cats come to sit outside the door, hearing activity within.

''Rita Jean?'' asks Harlan. ''Would you mind putting some of that corn-and-oyster pudding or whatever it is...''

And if this keeps going, dammit, I am going to run off. I mean it. You know what I got out of married life last week? A black eye!

''Where is my hatband?'' shouts Harlan. ''Did it grow legs or something?''

Before you run off anyplace, you got to figure out how to make money. One way to make money is snakes.

''Rita, I tell you something,'' says Harlan, wandering around the trailer in a pair of jeans. ''I am looking patiently for that snakeskin hatband.''

Rita Jean smashes eggs into the frying pan; butters toast.

There's truck gardening, but you need a truck patch. There's the bank, but you have to know how to work a computer. The rest of the jobs, I have to have a car to get there. Of course, there's selling all your stuff at auction, but I'd never figure out which stuff was mine and which was Mama and Daddy's and which was Harlan's, not to speak of my kid, his name's Joel, one of the happy little riders of that cutting horse called Married Life.

Rita Jean begins to imagine the entire horrendous scene of her escape from marriage:

And then if I got out there loading up all Harlan's stuff in the half-ton, he'd be on me like Grant took Richmond, throwing it back out on the ground.

Harlan would burst out the door, shouting, "What the hell are you *doing?*" Then he'd scrabble wildly through the load. "Rita Jean, that there VCR is *mine!* Where you taking this?"

"I'm taking it to auction at Lyn Creek, in order to become solvent, so I can disappear into a 1979 Chevy and get a job."

And Harlan would shout, "Get that shit out of the truck and get it back into the house."

And Joel would yell, "Mama, I *hate* you! Me and Daddy hate you!"

Okay, we just run through that scenario, and we seen it would not work. Why do I want to leave? I ask myself.

She has turned on her daily soap opera, and the Stoddard Trash Ranch is full of the sounds of television dialogue and jaybirds.

I make up lists as to what I want to do and how come. I want to be a country-western singer, but I can't sing. I want to be rich and have a lot of horses. I found a book in the supermarket at Lebanon last week that told you how to marry a millionaire. One thing it said, see, was to take up photography and get to meet rich men by being a reporter for a magazine.

Rita Jean, granddaughter of Lula Belle

Rita Jean is off into a scenario, a mind movie. She is a Young Girl Reporter, she hobnobs. She is in a house with French windows and a swimming pool.

Rita Jean would say, "Well, sir, let me see, maybe we could take your picture over here by the pool, you know, for the glitter nairthang that's shining all over your home pool that would be kind of kindly like a backdrop for your head."

"Well, yes," the rich man would reply, "but then you'd get me backlit, you see. Ah..."

Rita Jean would fumble with a sort of, you know, kind of a big camera, and say, "Do you know where it is you press on this camera?"

The rich man would say, "What magazine did you say you worked for?"

"Um, *Good Housekeeping?*"

"I don't think I..."

"It's got all these dumb recipes for hamburger mash and boiled tuna chips or something..."

"Wait a minute. Wait just a minute," the rich man would say.

That was the dumbest book I ever read. Telling women how to catch themselves a millionaire; it made me ashamed to be a member of the female species. You see, my imagination falls apart. I can't imagine it good enough to fill in the details. Maybe I got to work more on my imagination.

And here she is in the house after all — a double-wide at the edge of the woods with all the glittery soap operas — *Dallas* and *Dynasty.*

The phone rings.

"Stoddard's Mule Barn," says Rita Jean.

"Rita Jean?" says her mother, over in the other house, "I wish you'd quit answering the phone weird."

"I'm just entertaining myself."

"Are you all going to church or not?"

"Harlan ain't up to it," says Rita Jean.

"Why ain't Harlan up to it?"

"He sat up till five playing poker with Hugh Vaughn and some other guys and combing his mustache."

"Rita Jean," sighs her mom, "what are you going to do with that man?"

"Shoot him."

"And then what?"

"Take him to the rendering plant. And get him rendered."

Her mother, who can see Rita's place from her own front window, persists. She hasn't seen any church activity at Rita's for a long time.

"I wish you'd come to church," she says. "Brother Dwayne is going to talk about how the pioneers come here in the old days…"

And Rita Jean can nearly hear the old hymns, the elders standing up to testify…

"…and come into the Ozarks and the privations they had to endure and all like that."

"Well, I appreciate that, Mama, I really do."

"And how they had to wear old hogskin moccasins, and made their chimbleys out of mud and sticks, and kept their faith in the Lord. It was really a most amazing thing."

"It's wondrous."

"Well, it really is."

"It's awesome."

"And you ain't even going to come?"

"I don't guess he's going to tell how Marcus Poole went and set up the first still in Camden County, is he?"

Rita goes out to sit on the little porch, and the voice of the King of the Rattlesnakes speaks to her:

I looked for you, but you weren't there. I wanted you, and I looked for you, and in the place where your voice was to be, there was nothing.

The place where Harlan works is Rimrock Junction, that's a kind of phony western town they set up on Highway 50, just after you pass Bagnall Dam on the Lake Of The Ozarks.

A solid stream of cars flow down Highway 50 from all over the Midwest, heading for woods and cool water; city people.

They have an olde-tyme movie house, and they have these staged western gunfights, like this phony bank robbery, and Harlan plays the sheriff. He's supposed to come out of the saloon and see these robbers, and yell, "Hold it!"

"If you'll come around, ladies and gentlemen," shouts the announcer at the crowd of tourists in the Main Street, "we're going to see a re-creation of the last gunfight of the James Gang in Northfield, Minnesota when the James Brothers were gunned down in the midst of the Northfield Bank Robbery!"

More cars turn into the big parking lot; everything smells like raw oak siding.

"Stand back there by the saloon and general store, please," says the announcer. "The James Gang is just coming out of the bank, and the sheriff..."

Harlan — tall, skinny and black mustached — walks out of the saloon, and pauses for a blink. He sees the bank robbers exiting from the bank with big sacks that have $$ printed on them; they have bandannas over their noses.

"Hold it!!" shouts Harlan.

But of course they never held it. They never held it. They just robbed the hell out of that bank for the tourists every day at ten o'clock and two o'clock. They had to go rob the train and the stagecoach too. I'd bring Harlan's lunch, some baloney samwiches, and I'd drink about four Pepsi's and watch my husband blow away three guys.

"Hold it!!" Harlan shouts, again and again, four times a day.

"You'll never get us, sheriff!" shouts Hugh Vaughn, one of the bank robbers whose job it is to die, and then shoots back with smoky blanks out of a great big Gatling gun of a pistol.

"We're taking these greenbacks to Missouri!" yells Hugh Vaughn.

"The hell you are!" says Harlan, and steps forward bravely, firing a sawed-off. And Hugh Vaughn collapses, spouting out of his mouth a mixture of chocolate milk and red food coloring.

Rita Jean hears the train whistle and the rumbling coach and the cars honking.

All this gunfighting and arrgghhing would start at eight-thirty and it would already be ninety-five degrees. All the

127

lucky people who worked there and had these wonderful jobs would be coming in — the woman who ran the general store that sold all this Ozark junk for the tourists, little salt and pepper shakers that looked like little outhouses and said Ma and Pa; real Ozark honey from Pennsylvania; the engineer that drove the train; the girls that danced the Can-Can in the saloon — all of them in a fuss about their mama babysitting and getting their husband's lunches. There were twenty-two horses for tourist rides; soon as the first guns went off, they knew it was feed time.

"The hell you are!" screams Harlan. Guns go off and the horses impatiently neigh and paw at the ground. The red-clay dirt in front of the hitchracks has long trenches pawed into it.

I wanted to get a job there too, but they were all taken.

Rita and Harlan meet out in the parking lot by their truck. She has brought him his lunch. They lean against the pickup and drink soda pop. Joel is at home gunning his A.T.V. around the pond.

Harlan wipes his face in the glassy sunshine and goes to sit in the cab. "Rita Jean, don't you think when it gets to be ninety, ninety-five, we could ask for a day off? Man, it gets hot shooting that damned double-barrel, and I'm afraid the heat's going to warp it. And Peterson says I can't take off this damn claw-hammer coat, either. I told him we didn't want to rob that train twice, but he says that's how come the tourists take the train, is to get robbed. I look about as ugly as homemade sin by four o'clock."

The whole place glitters; windshields, bottle caps. Rita goes to sit in the other side. "Tell him," she says, "if it gets to be ninety-five the powder'll blow up in the barrel."

He has said this before. She has said this before. Nothing changes.

"I *told* him," snorts Harlan.

"Well, I don't *know*, Harlan. How come I got to think of everything?" says Rita Jean. She lets her head fall back, puts on her sunglasses.

"Well, the damn barrel gets hot."

"Well, throw it in the horse-trough!"

And there Harlan is again, a performing bear for tourists, a pseudo-armed Ozarkian, a professional redneck waving a sawed-off 12 gauge.

"Hold it!!" he yells, and all the gunpowder goes off at once and tourists scream and Hugh Vaughn spouts his chocolate milk and red food coloring. They get up after the applause and stand together for photos.

"Someday, this thing's going to kill me," says Harlan to Hugh Vaughn.

A tourist comes up to them, "Excuse me, could I take your picture? Could you put your arm around Katherine?" And so he does. Harlan is by far the more photogenic of the two; Hugh Vaughn wanders off.

"It's a very convincing gunfight," says the tourist. "We all screamed."

"Well," says Harlan, nodding vaguely, "we make everything authentic, that's for sure."

"Have you lived here in the Ozarks all your life?" asks the tourist.

Harlan shakes his head slowly and says, "Not yet."

The mornings are blue with haze in mid-July. Rita Jean has her few private moments on the porch, looking down toward Little Blue Spring. She is thinking:

And I looked for you, and I listened, but you weren't there. You weren't there in the evenings when I stood on the porch, looking down the hill, down into the valley of the Little Blue Spring, and you were not there in the mornings, when I got out of my bed at dawn, and the mist laid down carefully like the world's nightgown, and I wanted you, and you weren't there.

"Rita Jean? Rita Jean?" says Harlan, wandering out, "did you get that truck gassed up last night?"

Joel comes out too, shirtless, holding the kitten.

"What?" says Rita Jean. "No, I forgot. Joel, wear that blue bowling shirt, honey."

Joel hates the blue bowling shirt. He squeezes the kitten until it shrieks. He watches his parents.

"Dammit," says Harlan, "we're going to run out of gas and end up hitchhiking to work!"

And July grinds on toward August.

The Ozarks, like everyplace else in the world, are alive with electronic voices which implore, and order, and interrogate; they intrude and insist. The Ozarks have succumbed.

A P.A. system screams: "The helicopter rides leave every half hour! A view of the Ozark's you'll never forget!"

And its screams collide with, "Paragliding! Paragliding over Lake Of The Ozarks at Benson's Landing!"

And the radio promises, "Ozarks Arts and Crafts at the Camden County Craft Fair! Storytelling, Horseshoeing, Exhibitions!"

But there are always cassette tapes, Steve Fearing's "Jesse And Zee," and the private voice in your head.

I'll tell you a story that my grandma told me. It was a story that her grandmother told her, and it's about the King Of The Rattlesnakes. Her grandmother was named Maggie Johanna Burnett, and Maggie Johanna was a witch-woman. And one night she was sitting by the fire, in front of an old mud-and-stick chimbley, wearing hogskin moccasins, and a rattlesnake come to her door. And he said:

"Would you kindly let me come in, and warm myself by your fire?"

And Maggie Johanna said alright. So the rattlesnake, oh God it was a big rattlesnake, it was a timber rattler with a head on him like a flour cannister, I mean he was too big to be a snake and too small to be the Mississippi, but Maggie Johanna said, "Come on in. But you hide yourself in that corner over there. I got company coming, it's the deacon from the church, he's been out digging a grave for somebody that's died."

And the snake, because he was bashful and kind of easy set back before company, hid there just close enough to get warm.

It was October 31st, 1857, at ten-fifteen in the evening. And so the deacon came in and said, "Maggie Johanna! I just got the worst scare of my life!"

And Maggie Johanna said, "Well, what happened?"

And the deacon says, "I was out there digging Samuel Burnett's grave, with a lantern, because they got to bury him tomorrow, and I didn't get to it till late, because I was out fixing that fence the hogs busted through, and I was digging away there, and here come a whole congregation of rattlesnakes! It was a river of rattlesnakes!"

"Why, Lord save us," says Maggie Johanna.

And the deacon says, "Hang on, it gets worse. These rattlesnakes were carrying with them a coffin, and on the coffin was a silver crown. And they come slithering up to the gravehole and they says to me:

"'Get out of that gravehole.'"

And the deacon said, "So, Maggie, I tell you what, I got out!"

And the snake in the corner, when he heard the deacon say that, he gave a small rattle and a very small hiss, like somebody stepping on an air-brake. And the deacon said that these snakes all started lowering that coffin with the silver crown into the gravehole, and they said:

"Tell Thomas George that George Thomas is dead!"

And the deacon said: "And I said, 'What? What'd you-all say?'"

And the snake gave an even louder hiss over there in the corner by the fire. And the other snakes, the ones in the story, hung down like ropes, lowering the coffin with the silver crown down, down into the gravehole. And they all whispered in their many snake voices:

"Tell Thomas George that George Thomas is dead!"

And the big rattler in the corner gave another rattle, like the sound you hear before you die, like a rifle being loaded. And the deacon said:

"Maggie Jo, what is that? How can I tell Thomas George that George Thomas is dead if I don't know who Thomas George is?"

And the giant rattlesnake came slithering out of the corner, like a roll of dimes, like a bolt out of a bolt-hole, and reared up before the fire and said:

"What! Old George Thomas dead? Then, by God, I'm the King Of The Snakes!" and he vanished up the chimbley and was never seen again, except from time to time, a hundred feet long, with a head on him like a flour cannister, and he lives on the edges of the hayfields in summer when the men are haying, for the mice that come running away from the balers, and back in the very far country where the tourists never go, and the range of his wandering is from Eminence to Cross Timbers, from Fairdealing to the Marais des Cygnes. I don't tell that story too often, I guess we're just too used to watching Dynasty, *rich people accusing each other of dirty real things, and getting bad news on the telephone.*

And so the telephone rings a compelling blast, a spoiled brat, screaming for attention from anonymous distances.

"Oliver North Savings and Loan Company, may I help you?" says Rita Jean.

"Rita Jean," says her sister Tamara, "what's this about catching snakes?"

"Tammy! Babe! Listen, honey, they use them for hatbands and wallets. They'll pay thirty dollars a pound! Don't you think it's a good idea?"

"Sometimes," groans Tamara, "I think we found you wandering along the side of the road somewhere."

"Listen, I know where all these rattlesnakes are, it's a cinch, it's a *cakewalk*."

"Why don't you just get a *regular job*?" Tamara says.

"I got to get a car first, honey, a *car*. So I can get to one. Right now it's pure local enterprise."

"Okay, how do we do this? Rita Jean, you know this is illegal."

"It's easy, you just make snake-catchers out of waterpipe and wire... I know it's illegal. Don't bug me."

They are wandering in the cool nighttime woods, hoping for a copperhead. They have flashlights and gloves and high hopes. Joel has come along — they couldn't lock him in the house, after all.

"Now, Joel, you stay behind me, hear?" says Rita Jean. "If you get near any of these snakes, I'll bite you myself."

The flashlights make the woods seem alive. They know their way around, but it still looks alive. No snakes. Joel gets bored.

"Can I go down to the creek?" he says.

"I want you to stay here where I can keep an eye on you," says Rita Jean, grabbing his arm. "There's *snakes* around here."

Tamara is tipping over limestone tablets beside the wet-weather spring in the little hollow. "You just poke under these side rocks, Reet, they're always slithering around under...Never there when you want them, are they? Stepping on the damn things..."

"Tammy," whispers Rita Jean, "You ever fall in love?"

Tamara shines her light in Rita's face. "Rita, are you cheating on Harlan?"

"Joel, honey," says Rita Jean, letting go of his sleeve, "why don't you go down and play in the creek. Take the flashlight."

"No, *sir*. Not on your life," says Joel, who can't wait to hear the rest of this. "There's *snakes* around here."

Rita Jean shoves him. "You go on down there, honey, and catch some crawdads. For fish bait."

"They're eating them now," says Tamara. "It's cajun cooking. They're calling them crayfish." She's still turning over limestone slabs. "Them cajuns must be awful damn hungry. Joel, go on down there and catch some slimy crawdads; maybe I'll cook them for your daddy. In Vaseline."

"Looks like I ain't going to get to hear this," says Joel, reluctantly.

"*Move*," says Rita Jean.

"Alright, alright," he says, and crashes off through the buck-brush.

Tamara waits until she is sure Joel is out of earshot and turns to Rita, whispering fiercely, "You're *cheating* on him, and he's going to give you another *black eye*. Rita, you're going to get yourself beat up!"

"I am *not* cheating on him," whispers Rita Jean. "I don't

know anybody to cheat on him with, or I would."

"You'd *think* a person would have fallen in love with their husbands."

Rita Jean is suddenly seized by regret, as people are when they are on the brink of dissolving a marriage, recalling what it was, the fatal impulse, that led them to the altar with the wrong partner. "Oh, God, when I first saw Harlan, he was gorgeous, he was so yummy. Playing steel guitar in that band in Osage Beach. And I was sitting there drinking a Black Russian, fat as a Greyhound bus in that cherry red pants suit. I always wanted to look like Cher, you know? And, oh well. Harlan's forty-eight years old and he's got a mustache, and *he* looks more like Cher than I do. And you know damn well if I get a job, he'll go on part-time and let me support all three of us."

Tamara looks around for a solution like she looks for snakes; maybe solutions *are* like snakes — simple, slick, deceptive. "Has he looked around for another job?"

"Hell, no. He'll stay there and *shoot people* till he *dies*," says Rita Jean. She roots with her primitive digging-stick among leaves and sticks and acorns.

"You're an accident waiting to happen, Rita," says Tamara, shaking her head.

Rita Jean comes up with a grape-ivy vine, shines her flash on it and throws it away. "I tell you what, if he hits me one more time I'm going to put real bullets in Hugh Vaughn's gun, and then I'll be forty years in prison serving life without parole."

"There! There, get him, Reet!" says Tamara, suddenly seeing an evaporating set of coils.

"Woooo, he's a big one!" shouts Rita, as she runs to plant her boot on it.

THE SNAKE

Tom Byatt from Nacogdoches is coming on Saturday with a load of horses.

Rita Jean backs off as Tamara jumps in and lands on it with both sneakers. She says irrelevantly, "You know, this guy called Thomas Byatt is coming in Saturday with a loan of dude horses for the Junction..."

"*Help* me with this *snake,* Rita!" shouts Tamara.

"That's the biggest snake I ever saw!" says Rita Jean.

"In the *bag,* get him in the *bag,*" screams Tamara, as she holds out the tow-sack. "THE BAG!!!" And then he's in the bag.

Joel walks back up from the creek. He is angry and afraid. Maybe he'll go tell his father; it would make him feel adult, carrying tales. He can follow the path in the moonlight; a moon boy.

At Rimrock Junction, the air is blue with gunpowder and heat, carbon monoxide and electronic statements. This is how Harlan makes a living. He yells, "Hold it!"

And this is how Hugh Vaughn makes a living. He pauses, defiant, and yells, "You'll never get us, sheriff! We're taking those greenbacks to Missouri!"

And Harlan yells back, aiming, "The hell you are!" And so they make their living.

But in the evenings, five miles back on a country road, away from Highway 50 and the hotels and the condos, the paragliding and helicopter rides and speedboats on the lake, five miles back in the country, you could almost believe it wasn't there. They sit out on the steps of the little porch, in as little clothes as possible: Harlan, shirtless and barefoot, cleaning his shotgun; Rita in a big skirt and halter top, her hair up in rubber bands.

"I swear this barrel's going to warp," says Harlan. "I fire this thing fifteen times a day, and when it's ninety-five, I mean really, God."

Rita Jean intones, ritually, "Throw it in the horse trough."

Harlan blows down the barrel and puts away the ramrod. "Rita Jean, you don't know what you're talking about. Sometimes I think they found you wandering on the side of the road somewhere."

Rita Jean repeats, mindlessly staring at the woods, "You know something? I don't know what I'm talking about." She pauses. "I never did know."

"Welp...let's go to bed, it's late," says Harlan, stretching.

"I don't want to go to bed. I want to sit out here. Mama and Daddy's lights are on. I reckon Daddy's going to get drunk. He's so sweet when he's drunk."

"Come on to bed, honey." He remembers they haven't slept together for two weeks.

Rita Jean shies away from him. "I'm going to sit out here and watch the moon come up and listen to Daddy sing "Shenendoah." By the time he's finished that bottle he always starts singing "Shenendoah." Rita Jean sings, sort of... 'Oh, Shenendoah, I love your daughter'..."

"So you're not going to bed," Harlan says, angrily.

Rita Jean seizes herself up, stares away from him, down at the ravine. "I don't want to sleep with you, Harlan. You come home when you feel like it, and maybe I don't feel like it. You fight dirty and you think slow and you spend your life firing blanks. If you ever hit me again, someday I'm going to put real bullets in Hugh Vaughn's pistol."

Harlan stands up, his hands on his hips. "Well, maybe you'd just like to pack up and get the hell out of here, then!"

Rita Jean stands up too. They have exploded into a fight so quickly they might have planned it. "Wait, you got it all backwards. This here is my daddy's farm and we're living in this house rent-free, and if anybody gets out of here it's *you.*"

Harlan snatches up the clean, empty 12-gauge, "Honey, if you're going to talk about putting bullets in guns, I could tell you a thing or two."

Rita Jean isn't afraid of him. "I already know both of them!" she yells back, and doors and hearts are slammed shut, and a boy listens, crying, and then he slams shut too.

A twenty-foot gooseneck horse-trailer is pulling into Rimrock Junction, towed by a big Ford pickup. The driver eases through and past the parking lot and down to the stables. This is where somebody should say

Hello, Stranger. New in Rimrock, aren't you?

or ain't you but they don't. The stranger gets out of the pickup and goes back to check his horses through the slats; they are all standing. People all over the place — gawking tourists — but nobody who knows what to do with a load of horses. He is wearing a straw Resistol cowboy hat and $200 spurs, his jeans and boots are worn threadbare on the inside of the leg but nobody passing by has the sense to read any of these signals. Except our heroine, who looks at him and bites the apple once again.

Tom Byatt starts backing out the first horse. "Cope, cope, cope...Hey, ma'am, do you work here? Give me a hand would you mind? They's supposed to be somebody here."

Rita runs up to take one horse from him as he backs out another. "How far you come with these?" she asks.

"Today? Pine Bluff, Arkansas," Tom says. They begin to tie up horses on the hitch rails. Rita Jean is good with horses, Tom notes.

"Isn't anybody here to help you?" Rita says.

Tourists continue to stare. A child yells, "Hey, look at the horses!"

"They's supposed to be," says Tom, looking her over. "What are *you* doing here, just hanging around the parking lot?"

"My husband works here," says Rita. "He's the sheriff." She smiles at him, and he's just exactly what she always wanted, she thinks, but she thought that once before, but, you know...

And the King Of The Rattlesnakes whispers:

Isn't he wonderful, the way he leans on things, that Marlborough slouch, looking around for the right person to come up, walk into his life, say the right thing? I bet you didn't know he was from Nacogdoches and picks up killer horses.

Tom is still tying up horses. "One of those pretend sheriffs?"

Rita Jean checks her watch and lifts a forefinger. "Yup. There he goes now." And, in the distance, they hear Harlan shout "Hold it!" But, of course, they never hold it, they just go right ahead and she and Tom look at one another, listening to distant gunfire, screams, and the announcer.

Tom laughs. He walks another horse past her. "What do you-all do around here for entertainment?"

"Entertainment?" Rita is startled. Her whole life is one big entertainment. "Entertainment. You like catching snakes?"

Tom laughs again. "They *told* me not to come up to the Ozarks."

Rita has been busy. There have been frantic phone calls to borrow cars to deliver snakes to a place near Springfield; she has to run up new gypsy skirts on the sewing machine; and as she walks through the house she mentally separates Her Stuff from Harlan's Stuff, thinking *Someday*...There isn't much but there's always those old encyclopedias and the chain saw...and if she is the first one to bolt from the marriage, can he have her arrested or what? She has taken to writing in a diary and hiding it; she has taken to avoiding her mother in the other house across the field.

And Joel has begun to skulk, listening at doorways. His parents don't love one another now and maybe they never did, but they have loved him. He has been the sole love object in this mismatch and it has been a position of enormous power. At eight, he has often felt like a small, weak god as they vied for his attention and his love and he would bestow it on this one or that one, maybe for presents, or maybe for flattery. Now he senses that his mother has walked out of the game. Some of her attention has gone elsewhere. He would like to go and gossip with Nanny, draw her into a conspiracy against both of them, but a small voice of good sense says *you are only a child*. But he doesn't know any other game to play, and the game depends on the loveless marriage continuing, and he would have back again his power. His mother doesn't seem to care if he hints that he might love his dad better than her. She doesn't hear the hints. He can't seem to threaten her. She loves something, or somebody, outside the game.

Joel goes to the garden to pull weeds. It is still early enough to be cool; or, at least, the solid objects — the house, the porch, the geodes around the edge of the flower bed — have not absorbed enough heat to radiate it back at him. Joel loves conspiracies. He is crying. Maybe he only thinks he loves conspiracies.

Rita Jean has spent an entire thirty minutes doing her hair and putting on make-up. She imagines herself someone on *Dynasty* only not quite so shallow or mindless. She wishes she had a quill pen.

I can't be guilted, it's impossible. Or embarrassed, either. People asked me how I got that black eye and I told them I just loved listening to country-western on the radio, I love it so much I hit myself in the face with the radio.

She hears Joel yell from outside, "Mamaaaaa!"

Be quiet, Joel, she either yells or thinks or writes. I just feel so mean and hard sometimes, but you got to have some strength to get through life, don't you? I listen to the radio and I get this wonderful mournful story of somebody drinking their brains out in Puerto Vallarta, alone, alone, margaritas, nostalgia, here I am wearing these radio voices like a head-set, an innocent abroad, hard on the outside, soft on the inside.

143

Joel shouts, "Mama, I mean it!"

"Joel, I am writing in my secret diary," Rita calls through the window.

"Yeah," shouts Joel, "but come here quick!"

Rita Jean is furious. "Joel, I am going to lock you in the old warshhouse if you interrupt me One More Time when I am writing important thoughts in my secret, never-to-be-published diary!"

Joel's voice is nearer the window, pleading. "Yeah, but mama, I was cutting, see, I was cutting the fescue with the corn knife and I cut my finger off!"

In the corridor of the small local hospital in Lebanon, Rita sobs into the pay phone.

"Tammy, I will never, never, *never* write in that damn diary again. The doctor's trying to stick it back on but it ain't going to stick. Of course I'm calling from the emergency ward! Oh, in Lebanon. Go tell Harlan at the Junction! Tell him to get down here."

And now Joel is in bed, sleeping, with Harlan sitting at the bedside and Rita at the door. They stare at one another over the cowboy designs on the coverlet, sad and furious.

The phone rings. Rita says, "Persian Gulf Oil Delivery, can you hold a couple of years?"

And the King Of The Rattlesnakes whispers over the lines:

But how beautiful you are, and how light in spirit, and I have seen you walk to the spring for water in the heat of the day, and your voice is beautiful as well, it is light and pleasing to me as springwater, and in the mornings, out of the expanding mists of the Gasconade, and the martins scalloping the air, I have seen you looking for flints in the shallows, looking for the bird arrowheads and the deer arrowheads, that the old people have left there for you, and all that was edged in them, all that was lethal is gone; you are the woman who invented zero, by counting on your fingers, and there was one finger less every time.

Rita Jean and Tamara are sitting on the front porch, and Rita is tearing her diary out page by page, wadding up the pages and stuffing them into the burn barrel. She thinks,

Nobody can really tell about their own lives, you always have a blind spot about yourself that you can't see, that's how come you need your relatives; boy, they'll tell you... and

you say, "Well, what did other people do in a time like this?"
and they'll tell you that, too, in excruciating detail, and you
say, "Well, maybe I'm just normal."

"Rita Jean," says Tamara, "you are walking headling into sheer trouble, you're looking for the perfect non-existent man and if he don't come around, you're going to make him up."

"But I want him," says Rita. "That's what I want."

"People in hell want ice water, too."

Rita Jean nods. "There's some in the refrigerator, honey, in the Mason jar."

Rita Jean is sitting with Tom at a little tavern in Camdenton, where there are neon beer signs and people are playing shuffleboard. She feels guilty and happy and afraid and she is not caught up in a perpetual win-lose tug-o-war with her spouse and her child and she likes it.

Tom is saying, "Well, I just run horses back and forth across the country. Trucks, horses."

"What do you think about when you drive?"

"Hm. I guess between Nacogdoches and Texarkana I was thinking about problems. Problems at home."

But that's the last thing Rita wants to hear about. "What about the rest of the way?"

Tom laughs. "It's funny what you do with your mind."

"Like what?" Rita knows what she does with *her* mind. Maybe other people are weird too.

"Like repeat conversations in your head so you come out sounding better than the other person. You do that too.

Open up your hand.''

''There isn't anything in it.'' She lays her hand on the table between them, palm upward.

Tom looks. ''No.''

''Can you read palms?''

Tom reaches out, as if her hand were a small book, opens it. ''Well, let's see. Looks like you died at the age of seven.''

Rita Jean catches his fingers. ''Let me read yours,''

''All you can see there is a lot of steering wheels and rope burns...let's not.'' He smiles and keeps one hand in his lap.

''Can you make a living at it? My boy's interested in horses; but he just lost a finger. Can you do that work with nine fingers?''

''Okay, read my palm.'' He puts his right hand on the table.

''Oh, me and my big mouth. How'd you lose two fingers?''

Tom thinks for a minute and decides to tell her something about his missing fingers. Of course, he has been asked many times. ''Well, I'll tell you a story about that. When I was in the service, I was out in San Francisco, me and some other officers decided we were going to enter some bullfrogs in the Jumping Frog contest of Calaveras County. So what we did was, we called up this general in Oklahoma and told him the honor of the outfit was at stake, you see, and for him to get some bullfrogs for us. We told him that Oklahoma bullfrogs were the test pilots of the frog world, that, man, they had the right stuff. It was mainly just to get this general out slopping around in the mud. We didn't care for him a great deal. And damned if

he didn't put them on a special shipment on a plane out to
us. It was about a month before the contest, so we decided
to freeze them? like, put them into hibernation? This
fellow from a chemical lab, research stuff, said he'd freeze
them for us, and I tell you what, he froze them good.
Liquid nitrogen. So when he took them out of storage, he
tripped, and they all *broke*. But I kept one in the refrigerator, I didn't trust this guy. He was sort of wacko. The one
in my refrigerator would kind of wake up a little, crawl
around. I guess the racks were hard on his feet. I found
him on the mustard one time, another time he was down
on the bok choy. But he wasn't broke, anyhow. So we
entered him.''

Rita Jean laughs. ''Did you win?''

''Nope.'' He keeps on looking at her. He is much older.
He realizes they will tell each other all about each other.
They will go to a motel. They will buy land somewhere.

Rita Jean persists. ''What's this got to do with losing
your fingers?''

''Not a damn thing.''

Rita Jean smiles at him. ''Tom.''

Tom gets up and comes to take her by the elbow. ''You
going to dance with me or what?''

And the next morning, in the shimmering heat and
crowds and a claw-hammer coat, Harlan screams,
''Hold it!''

And Hugh Vaughn sneers wildly, ''You'll never get us,
sheriff!'' and fires the enormous pistol, bellowing, ''We're
taking these greenbacks to Missouri!''

And is he? By God? "The hell you are!" roars Harlan and the double-barreled 12-gauge goes off and a big clot of dusty wadding flies out and smacks Hugh Vaughn in the eye. Harlan smiles nastily through the smoke, and Hugh Vaughn staggers around, furious. The crowd gives them a big hand.

"Harlan! Have you gone out of your mind? You done hit me with the wadding! What are you stuffing in that gun?"

Harlan says, up close, "Are you seeing my wife on the side, Hugh Vaughn?"

Hugh Vaughn paws at his eye, "I ain't seeing her on the side, or on the front, or from behind, man. You watch what you stuff in that gun, or I'm going to be loading mine with rock salt and nails."

And the P.A. system intones, "Ladies and gentlemen, that was the true-life re-creation of the Dalton gang's shoot-out in Coffeyville, Oklahoma."

"It was Kansas, you turkey," snarls Harlan under his breath and then they smile at the crowd and pose for photos.

Rita is in the privacy of her mind, of not her diary. She reviews herself, her life and her ancestors.

My great-grandmother was a midwife, her name was Nannie Hanlin, and she never took money, but people would give her gifts. My aunt has a bowl that somebody gave Nannie; it has beautiful leaves and vines on it. Mama was just telling me this the other day; it was the most amazing thing.

And her mother had said, "Rita Jean, I just wrote some things down for you here. This here was your granddad's song; he could sing every verse of it, even up to when he was so old...and about Nannie, too."

Rita Jean is disturbed. "Mama, why are you giving me this? You feeling okay these days?"

Rita's mother, retiring and faded, drifts back to her house across the field. "I just want you to have this, honey. Did you know me and your Aunt Cissy used to sing on the radio? In 1936?"

And they said she would go even in the dead of night to deliver a baby, and saved so many of them, some were blue and some were breathless and some had cords wrapped around their necks; but she disentangled them and blew their breaths back into them and laid them in warm water until they were red as stop signs and screamed like guinea-hens. And one time some poor people whose baby she'd saved, they said, what do you want for payment? And she said, nothing, don't bother about it. And they insisted. And she said, oh, oh well, when I die, you put a red rose on my grave every year. And there is a red rose on Nannie Hanlin's grave every year to this day. The baby she saved is eighty-nine years old. Their names are Moorehouse. It's a fire rose, the old kind, that grew in my grandmother's yard.

Joel stands at the garden gate. "Mama?"

Rita Jean leaps up from her cookbook. "Yes, darling? Sweetheart? Mama's baby love, my lamb, nine-fingered joy of my heart?"

Joel holds his injured hand in the other and asks, "We going to go catch some more snakes?"

"Not for a while, honey," Rita says, "your hand has to get better."

"We could go and catch snakes and talk."

"About what, Joel?"

"Dad ain't hardly home anymore." Joel won't look at her.

"Well, maybe me and your dad are going to live in different places for a while."

"Was it because I cut my finger off?"

"Oh, honey, *no*, don't ever think that."

150

"It doesn't look very nice." He holds up his bandage.

Rita Jean says, against all logic, "It looks perfectly fine! You can't even tell! Listen, want to go see a man who's got eight fingers? You don't even notice it." She edges toward confessions.

Joel is suspicious. "What does he do?"

"Sells horses and trades stock, and one thing and another. He's from Texas. He's up here a week or so looking to buy some stock." She smiles, abject, hoping.

Joel shouts, "*No!* No, I don't want to see him. He's probably a jerk, or he wouldn't of lost his fingers!"

Everything was going wrong. Everything. Me and Tamara had just got seven hundred dollars from the snakes, and selling all this stuff at auction, half of which we stole out of daddy's barn, and it had to go for Joel's finger, because Harlan had let the insurance lapse. Mama's giving me this family history and stuff that makes me scared she's got something fatal, and Joel wants a dirt bike! And if I don't get it for him he'll go live with his daddy. And Harlan's going to get lawyers or something, and it's all just us peaceful country folks down here in the Ozarks. You know, nothing ever happens. And I can't stop thinking about Tom from Nacogdoches. Like it was out of a movie. I started imagining all this stuff in my head, making it up, man. I was radioactive.

"Rita Jean," the imaginary Tom says, "you're about the most attractive woman I ever met, honey, you are radioactive. Come, darling, leap into my four-wheel drive with the ripped upholstery and the bumper sticker that says SHIT HAPPENS *and we shall..."*

And then I've been reading all these international spy novels, that just made it worse.

The imaginary Tom whispers, "If you're going to travel with me, my dear, I suggest you pack lightly, because I travel fast, and my purposes are, of course, obscure, and I may look like I am unimpeachably blank for the better part of the day but I assure it's a very good vintage..." and his voice becomes serpentine. "As for jumping frogs, I have always found them delicious, fried in Vaseline; it's cajun cooking, please ignore the peculiar sharpness of my teeth..."

And there he is, she thinks, grasping, forbidding, earthbound.

Harlan shouts, in the distance, "Hold it!" and she drifts over to the stables where Tom is looking at Coggins Test results.

"Did you find what you wanted up here?" says Rita Jean.

"Yes. No. Sort of. How come you took off early and left me playing the jukebox?" Tom puts his hat back on.

"Because of Joel."

"Oh. Of course." He shuffles papers.

"What'd you do after I left?"

"I got so drunk I couldn't have hit the wall with a handful of beans."

"How come?"

"I wanted you, and I had some things to say to you, and I wanted to listen to you."

"People in hell want ice water."

"I know that. What do you do about life and sex and everything?"

"I get by. I make up things in my head." And she thinks, *if you only knew, cowboy.*

"I know that one, too. When are you going to stop just getting by?" He reaches over and pulls her earring as if it were the doorbell to her head.

"I think I am going to put real bullets in Hugh Vaughn's guns one of these days and spend the rest of my life peacefully in jail. Joel will come visit me. I'll escape. In the laundry truck..."

Tom shakes his head. "Don't talk about that kind of intention. Don't even say it. You don't know what you're talking about, and, if you did, you'd wish you didn't. I don't know if that makes sense or not."

Rita and Tamara are at Tamara's trailer on the other side of Camdenton. Rita Jean knows gossip is flying around among local people — about her fights with Harlan, and about her two evenings out with Tom Byatt; about her scandalous behaviour. She feels guilty and exultant and free. Her Aunt Mollie has been on the phone as usual. Mollie is an expert scandal sheet. Her favorite *technique,* Rita thinks, *I know her favorite technique. She calls family long distance and exaggerates, and fetches out half-truths over several hundred miles, so nobody can really confirm,*

and it's like part true, and people love repeating it, these damn Missouri small towns. She calls my niece and screams, "Oh, my God, Rita left Joel alone and made him chop corn and he cut off two fingers and near bled to death while she was out with one of her boyfriends!" And my niece has told five people before she finds out it wasn't quite the truth but who cares? And Mollie calls Mama and screams, "Oh, my God, Ethel, Harlan's goin' to court and have Rita arrested for child abuse because of that finger!" He's gone to the court for something, though. He says I'll find out. Oh, I don't care, I don't care... And so she has come to laugh and talk with her sister, somebody who's on her side, and they gossip among Tamara's college texts and collection of old second hand dishes, while the kids play in the pond.

Tamara says, "Remember that time Mama and me and you and Aunt Cissy raced Daddy and them to Grandpa's house? Two hundred miles."

"That was insane," laughs Rita Jean. "All the women and girls in one car and the guys in the other...remember when Cissy passed them on the right side of the road?"

"God, I thought they were going to go off the Jack's Fork bridge," laughs Tamara. "Cissy'd try anything. Cissy showed me how to put on lipstick, and blot it on letters. Like kisses. Letters to Him, whoever He was at the moment."

"Remember when we had to kill those two hundred chickens? It was the slaughter of the innocents."

"That was Mama's idea for making money. The things

a person does to make money! And here your seven hundred dollars went for Joel's..." (she starts to whisper) Joel's finger. Are those kids hanging around the door?"

Rita whispers back, "No, no they're down at the pond. Why am I whispering? But don't even talk about it Tammy, that was his *finger*. The money doesn't matter."

Tamara snorts. "You'd think Harlan could fill out a damn insurance form! Seven hundred dollars for a finger that they didn't even try to stick back on! That's criminal!"

"They knew we didn't have any money or any insurance." Rita thrashes around in the chair, guilty. Sometimes, though, she wonders if Joel might have done it on purpose? That's even worse.

"One last idea," says Tamara, getting her attention.

"It's no use," says Rita, "they already threw it away."

"No, that's not what I meant. Enter that storytelling contest next week. They're going to have it at the arts and crafts festival and all you have to do is sit up there and tell stories like you do all the time anyhow!"

"But that's just *fun*. That's just *us*."

"Enter that storytelling contest next week. They're going to have it at the arts and crafts festival and all you have to do is sit up there and tell stories like you do all the time anyhow!"

But that's just *fun*. That's just *us*."

"You think 'cause it's fun it isn't serious? Tell about the time Daddy shot the refrigerator; tell about Bucky's dead squirrel dog; tell about Nannie Hanlin and the rose on her grave. Just run your mouth, Rita Jean, like you always do. It's just pouring out of you all the time; you might as well do something with it. Unless we're going to hook you to a generator."

"But I don't know how Nannie saved that baby," says Rita Jean. "Mama just heard about that she got the rose on her grave every year."

Tamara waves her hands impatiently. "Well, make it *up*! Haven't you got any imagination?"

Rita is alone at home. She doesn't have to look after Harlan anymore and she can wash dishes slowly.

I wished I'd seen some of them doing it before. Then I'd know if they wanted fairy stories or old-time fairy stories or real stories or what. And here I am with my marriage breaking up. Let's see... I got to do this so I can get a car so I can get a job so I can get some money and then I can do something about my marriage breaking up one way or another. Harlan's gone in for lawyers. Maybe I should get one. There goes the dirt bike money.

"Mama?"

"Yes, peg o' my heart, baby lamb?"

Joel says, slyly, "Maybe I want to go see that guy with the eight fingers." He has given her a small concession. He feels generous and powerful, seeing her gratitude. He wants his dirt bike. He loves her and the world is terrible.

And alongside this terrible world is the world of where you are invited to come. The King Of The Rattlesnakes whispers:

Yes, come on in. You can come in and sit here beside my fire, you on one side and me on the other, in front of this old mud-and-stick chimbley, and we will make a blaze and we will make a world, where we will remember the dead, and address the living, and in this world is the combustion of hearts of oak, and apples of paradise both sweet and poisoned, and that which is easy come by, and that which is forever lost. I have so many stories to tell you, so many things that have gone unheard for so long, and they are waiting. Tell Thomas Byatt that Byatt Thomas is dead.

Rita Jean and Tom Byatt lay entwined as one, underneath the willow of dreams, while the radio plays Shadowfax. They are in a motel north of the dam, an area so thick with tourists and hotels and water sports that it is anonymous. Rita feels as if she is drifting in warm water when she wakes up. She wants to be in love; the price is high. Life's mistakes have caused her furies and The Furies are expensive. She knows Joel is with his father but he will be back early in the morning. It seems they are waiting to catch her out, catch her falling in love.

She shakes Tom in his tangled sheets. She loves everything about him; his nose and his skin and low, slow voice, his reticent humor, his solidity. His war wounds and brown eyes.

"What?" he says.

She shakes him again.

"Tom? Tom? I have to get back."

"Yes," he says, struggling to wakefulness.

"Tom, you have to take me home."

"Yes, I do." He opens his eyes. "How come, baby?"

"Harlan's bringing Joel home this morning. I have to be there. If I'm not, he'll take me to court."

"I dreamed something, honey," says Tom.

"I know. You got up and moved that chair in front of the door and then came to bed again."

"Right," he says. "Yes, I do that sometimes."

"Tom..."

"Yes, baby, hand me my jeans."

In the small dressing room in the back of the Saloon at Rimrock, Hugh Vaughn and Harlan are getting on their 1890's clothes: the claw-hammer coat and stovepipe boots for Harlan, the plastic "leather" vest and bandana for Hugh Vaughn. Hugh Vaughn mixes up his chocolate milk and red food coloring. Harlan has been off to lawyers. He is discovering the joys of being the one left, the one who hung grimly onto a bad marriage until the other was forced out. The joys of self-righteousness and woundedness and blaming. He has become litigious. He has made legal moves; three at least. He has begun to speak of himself and his lawyer as "we." "We went to court" he has been saying. "We got an injunction." And "we're considering moves on child custody." He always says this in a modulated voice, quietly, regretfully, and nodding. Hugh Vaughn thinks he will throw up if Harlan nods and modulates and says "we" anymore. Harlan likes feeling cheated and hard-done-by, he likes phoning Aunt Mollie and any other of Rita's relatives who will listen, and repeating invented scandal, and real scandal, but, on the other hand, what about this falling in love shit? The chorus girls are shrieking and laughing in their dressing room next door.

"Hugh Vaughn," says Harlan, looking in the mirror, "do you think my mustache is getting too long?"

"Just load up, Harlan," sighs Hugh Vaughn.

"They ought to put a better mirror in these dressing rooms."

Hugh Vaughn loads his pistol. "You going to stand there and look at yourself all day?"

"You know something, the barrel on this here shotgun gets so hot on a day like this, I don't know if this thing's going to explode on me." Harlan wanders to the door.

Hugh Vaughn could weep with exasperation. "Well throw it in the damn horse trough!"

Joel has been driven to the parking lot by Rita Jean and sent over to the Saloon with Harlan's lunch. Maybe she will try to mollify him with food, maybe he'll have lunch and forget about the lawyers. Faint hope. But maybe Joel will be fooled into thinking his parents are friends and not cut off anymore fingers.

Joel walks through the grounds of Rimrock carrying the heavy black metal lunch bucket. In his visits with Harlan he has heard his father say his mother needs to be taught a lesson. He has heard his father talk about lawyers and jails and child custody. It all has to do with love, somehow. Doesn't it? Teaching lessons. He will teach his mother a lesson. If she loved him she would live with his father and they would argue, he would take sides, and then one or the other would buy him a dirt bike and they would all go to jail and live in the courtroom and the lawyers would bring them lunch. She apparently loves somebody else, though, and this other man can't be managed. He wants to see this other man; the other man needs to be taught a lesson. He needs to join in the game, the only game Joel knows. Joel bumps into tourists, dodges horses, clutching the lunch bucket.

159

Joel reaches the stables. "Are you Tom Byatt? From Texas? With the horses?"

Tom looks down. "That's my name. That's where I'm from."

"I'm Joel. My name's Joel Stoddard."

"I know that. You're Rita Jean's boy," says Tom.

Joel stands his ground. "Rita Jean is my mother and Harlan is my daddy. He's the sheriff."

"Yes, I know that." Tom stands by a pile of saddles, looking down at Joel.

"Mama said you only had eight fingers."

"That's right. See here? Hasn't slowed me down a bit."

Joel stares. "Well, how'd you lose them?"

"Um, I was in a war. Something blew up."

Joel lies, despairingly, with all his small intensity, "I come with my mama every day, she brings lunch to my dad. She brings him a nice lunch every day, like ham samwiches and Dr. Pepper and Fritos, and everything?

That's because she loves my daddy a lot. See, this is his lunch. I got it today."

"Yes," nods Tom, "she does, she loves your daddy a lot."

"She *does*, she *does*, and they kiss and everything!" says Joel, almost screaming. "I *seen* them!"

"Saw."

"I *saw* them and everything, it's because they *love* each other, and you better stay away from my mother, you hear what I said? You stay away from my mother, and quit talking to her! You stay away!!"

"Son, stop, hold on," says Tom, backing away.

"And my daddy's the sheriff!" cries Joel, "and he'll use that shotgun on you sure as you're standing there! You keep your truck away from our house!"

Tom puts his hands in his back pockets. "Alright, slow down. I won't come around." *At least, you won't see me,* he thinks. *You'll get used to it.*

Joel opens the lunch bucket, fumbling, "And I got my daddy's pistol, right here!"

Tom sees the pistol. "Joel, slow down, give me that." His hands come out of the back pocket. He holds out the mutilated hand, appealing.

"It's *loaded,* too," screams Joel, "it's *loaded!*"

Tom continues to hold out his hand. "I can see it's loaded. Point it at the ground, Joel. You know how to load and unload a revolver?" Did he survive Khe San to get shot by an eight-year-old?

Joel becomes sly, and powerful. "Yeah, I know, I watched my dad."

"Show me. I don't believe you. Point it at the ground."

Joel smirks. "Oh, yah? Look, like this..." He pulls the trigger, and as he does, hears his father's voice in the distance, *"The hell you are!"*

160

Rita and Tamara are in Tamara's trailer; clothes are all over the floor, a whippoorwill descants outside. Joel is with his father. There were shots and near misses and more lawyers.

"This is going to give me a heart attack," says Rita Jean.

"Don't get all tarted up, Rita Jean! Honey, take off those rhinestone earrings!" Tamara flips through *Glamour.*

Rita Jean throws the rhinestone earrings on the bed. "Well, how am I supposed to look? Earthy, Earth Mother, right? How about some shoes made out of bark, and mud necklaces, and horse blankets?"

"You know something of yours I always just *loved...*" says Tamara, looking up.

"You *stole* that green wool sweater dress!!" yells Rita.

"I did not. You gave it to me, I begged you and begged you and you gave it to me. Anyway, I left it in a motel in Memphis." Tamara roots around in a scarf drawer.

"That must have been Larry Otami," says Rita Jean.

"Try this. Hold still." Tamara has a paisley shawl.

"Well, what were you wearing *out* of the motel?"

"Horse blankets," says Tamara. "Hold *still.* I am trying to button this *up.*" Now Tamara has fastened a high-necked blouse on her. "You want to look like a tart? Harlan will get custody for sure."

"I told you to stay away from those rodeo guys," Rita says.

"If you ever, *ever*, EVER tell stories about me and that rodeo guy...and when is this Tom going back to wherever he come from?"

"I *repel* men, Tammy," sighs Rita Jean. "I send them off their feed or something. You think it's my big mouth? All of a sudden he says…"

Rita and Tom Byatt stand beside the driveway gate. There are evening sounds, whippoorwill, katydids, somebody singing "Shenendoah" off-key and slightly drunk in the distance. Tom's pickup is parked behind the stand of oak.

"Welp," says Tom.

"What do you mean, *welp*?" says Rita Jean and looks away. "What does *welp* signify?"

Tom laughs. "I guess the owner and manager of that place of entertainment is happy with the jar-heads I sold him for the tourist trade. I have another load near Fort Worth."

"Welp," sighs Rita Jean.

"Seeing as how I'm not into couple-busting."

"Okay. Well, if I don't see you before, you have a good Christmas." Rita Jean gives up.

"I wrote you a poem. Here." Tom reaches into his shirt and hands her a piece of paper.

"A *poem*?"

"Yeah, it rhymes. And it's embarrassing as hell, so don't never, never remind me of it."

"Can I read it now?" She starts to open it.

"Nope," says Tom, shaking his head. "It's mushy. Now, listen, give it a month or so and see if that boy of yours would like to come down and learn something about the care and feeding of large animals. He might not want to come. Give it a couple of months."

"Really?" Well, like, what should he have with him before he leaves out? I mean, should I buy him a saddle? Or something?" Rita Jean suddenly laughs with relief. She knows Joel has always been bribed, and it's wrong, but she doesn't know any other way.

"My mother used to say there's only two things you need in this world, honey," says Tom, "that's what she'd say, she'd say, all you need in this world is two things, money and blankets. And the rest is fortitude. Fort-itude. Itude."

"Like Fort Sill. Fort Itude."

"Itude...wasn't that a Mexican general?" Tom kisses her. He's ready to go.

At the storyteller's contest, Rita has spent an hour trying to calm herself in the alley behind the community hall. There are local people and tourists as well. She walks up on stage, shaking, sits down and says, "My name is Rita Jean Stoddard and I'm here to tell you the truth about my life; I might as well, nobody else will. And one thing is, I mean about my life, is all these stories that got passed down. And, of course, there's the real ones, like from now, but if I tell those, my relatives will kill me. So I can't tell you about my sister Tamara running off to Memphis with this rodeo guy..."

Tamara, in the audience, screams, "RITA JEAN!!!"

"Now," says Rita Jean, forging on, "I can either tell you about the time me and my sister and my cousins had to kill two hundred chickens, or I can tell you about the King Of The Rattlesnakes that come to visit my great-great grandmother, Maggie Johanna Burnett."

Somebody in the crowd shouts, "Running off to Memphis with the rodeo guy! Or with the man from Nacogdoches!"

Somebody else says, "King Of The Rattlesnakes!"

"What about the jumping frog that ate San Francisco? Or about the time daddy shot the refrigerator?" says Rita, grabbing wildly for stories. She's in a spotlight. She can't see anybody. She wonders if she will live.

"King Of The Rattlesnakes!" someone yells. And, lower, "I like that one."

Rita Jean gets hold of herself, tells herself this is just the Camdenton Community Hall, that her personal life is nobody's business, and says, "Well, one time in the winter, (maggie Johanna was very young then, too, and subject to flattery) and she was sitting beside the fire when there came a knock at the door. And it was a giant rattlesnake, I mean he was too big to be a snake and too small to be the Mississippi, and the snake said,

May I come in and warm myself, Maggie Johanna; may I come in and warm myself beside your fire? It is not you I want, Maggie Jo, but your great-great-granddaughter, and it will take me three generations, so many lost and wasted lives to get her, but I am slow, and I am careful, and I am thorough in my way. I have little to give you in return, not even money or blankets, but only sharp-edged flints, and apples both clean and poisoned, and that which is easy come by and then forever lost. You're a beautiful woman, Maggie Jo, and your voice is sweet and light, pleasing as springwater.

"And Maggie Jo said,

"Now, that's about the nicest flattery I ever heard, and it's a shame it won't work, because I am throwing you right out of this house.

And the snake said,

"The hell you are."